Write Off Line 2016
Everyone's a Winner

Edited by
Jean Gilbert and Chad Dick

RHP

www.roguehousepublishing.co.nz

First edition published in September 2016

ISBN 978-0-473-36966-8

Write Off Line 2016 contributors are Year 9 to 13 students of Ashburton College, Avondale College, Cashmere High School, Diocesan School for Girls, Epsom Girls Grammar School, Green Bay High School, Greymouth High School, Hauraki Plains College, Hornby High School, Kerikeri High School, Macleans College, Motueka High School, Mount Roskill Grammar School, Nayland College, Newlands College, Ngaruawahia High School, Pompallier Catholic College, Sacred Heart College Lower Hut, Sacred Heart Girls' College New Plymouth, St. Mary's College Wellington, Tauranga Girls' College, Twizel Area School, Wellington East Girls' College, and Whakatane High School.

Original Cover Design by Kodi Murray

Write Off Line 2016

Contents

Foreword

Write Off Line 2016 continues the series which aims to encourage and support young writers. We want to provide opportunities for secondary school students to not only practise their skills and receive feedback on their work, but also to become published authors. With this in mind, our annual writing competition allows us to bring together an anthology that shows the talent and imagination of the participants, and lets them experience the thrill of seeing their work in print.

For this, the fifth collection, we asked students to turn their imaginations inward, and focus on the theme of 'Everyone's a Winner'. Again, we were overwhelmed with submissions from more than thirty schools. In both poetry and prose, the students have surprised and delighted us, showing great skill in their use of words, and bringing humour, excitement, horror, and fascination to the page. In some cases, there is a darker element to the stories and, though we don't encourage what is depicted, we appreciate the gritty art of expression.

We wish we could have published more of the pieces, but sadly this was not possible. But all students received individual feedback, and we hope this encourages all to continue to write.

Running the Write Off Line competition involves considerable work and would not be possible without help. We are very grateful to Piper Mejia, who is the principal organizer of the event, and whose guidance has been invaluable. We have also received support from SpecFicNZ (**www.specfic.nz**) and Tauranga Writers (**www.taurangawriters.org.nz**) with the running of the competition. We also thank our judges, Jan Goldie and Emma Shi, for their hard work in both decision making and providing feedback, and artist, Kodi Murray, for his magnificent and inspirational cover design.

Jean Gilbert and Chad Dick

GIANNA LILL

The Disastrous Combination of my Nan and the Mall

I desperately hold the vomit in my mouth, as Nan races around the bend like a speeding bullet. I reckon I am experiencing enough G-force to knock a person out. From another driver's perspective, I can only imagine it would be unbelievably unnerving, seeing what at first appeared to be an enormous car with no driver, but just as you're passing it, you can see two beady eyes peering over the steering wheel.

Nan is probably too short to sit in the front seat with the air bag, let alone actually drive the car. She sits on the front edge of the seat (with the seat forward all the way), just so she can see out of the windscreen. She looks like a deranged 'Hunchback of Notre Dame'. She swerves past another car, shaking her wrinkly old fist at the driver. I cover my face in shame, as we curve anticlockwise round the roundabout. The horn blasts are still ringing in my ears as we enter the mall car park – via the exit.

Nan gets out of the car, rubbing her large, swollen nose. She reaches past my face to get the miniature backpack she always wears. I hold my breath as the cigarette fumes threaten to kill me. Nan adjusts the triangular orange-and-white striped scarf she wears over her head, as we go into the mall.

Nan is like an ancient baboon; a condescending expression is on her face, her mouth wide, her lips pursed.

She thinks she knows everything. 'Life experience!' as she says. I think it's more like 'Life experience which I can no longer remember.'

We walk into 'Farmers'.

"Do you remember what we're looking for?" she drones.

"We're looking for a Toy Story toy for my cousin."

"Good. I was just checking your memory."

Nan struts up to the shopkeeper and asks, "Do you have any Toy World here?"

The shopkeeper looks befuddled.

"You know, I think if we're trying to find Toy World, we probably shouldn't look for it in Farmers," I say with an exasperated sigh. "She means Toy Story."

We then find out that they don't have any Toy Story products, and we are directed to Toy World.

"See, G? I know what I'm looking for!" Nan chirps.

It reminds me of the time she was going on about how she was breaking her bad smoking habits.

"I'm so good now! Yesterday I had only one cigarette before breakfast, and I didn't have another ..."

"Go on."

"… until morning tea!"

I laughed so hard I cried. They say that New Zealand is going to be smoke free by 2020. I don't see that happening if Nan is still alive.

We wander up the block towards Toy World. Nan has this smile on her face: the same smile that a dog would have chasing a ball. She says that by the time we walk to Toy World and back we will have walked five kilometres. Obviously Nan's spatial awareness is as bad, if not worse, than her memory.

We reach Toy World and walk in. The bell sings of our presence, and a shopkeeper appears at the front desk. The dusty smell of the shop itches my nose.

"Hello. How may I help you today?" the shopkeeper asks.

Nan smiles pleasantly. "Hi there! Do you have any Toy World?"

I give another pained cringe.

"Erm, we are Toy World."

"She means Toy Story," I grumble.

The woman guides us over to the Toy Story section, and we end up buying a giant 'Woody' toy.

He better like it! I think, tired of having to put up with Nan's antics.

Back at the car park, I give a big sigh of relief that I can finally go home and collapse on the floor, thankful that I haven't died. Then I realise that there's still the car ride back. I look at Nan's creepy smile and feel a funny sensation inside.

My mother once told me that, whatever the situation, everyone is a winner. Now I can tell her that she is very wrong. That is if I even make it home alive.

The car door shuts.

The engine starts.

Nan heads towards the entrance.

Help.

A True Winner

"Checkmate."

That was the only word Tom had heard in the last three hours. He was preparing for a national chess tournament in a fortnight. His older sister, Lucy, was helping him, and had won at least twenty times. They had played in silence, apart for the occasional sigh from Tom.

"Ugh, I'm so bad," Tom groaned.

"No you're not," Lucy replied. "You're just not trying hard enough." She set the chessboard up again.

"Yeah, because I'm bad." Tom moved the pawn in front of his king two spaces forward.

"Look, if you don't try against me, you won't last five minutes in the nationals. Just because you aren't winning, doesn't mean you can't." Lucy's voice had a stern tone all of a sudden. "Besides, even if you've lost the game itself, you've won in trying, or you've succeeded in making someone proud." Lucy moved her knight.

Tom shrugged. "Maybe, but if you win, they'll be even more proud, and you also get the glory of coming first." Tom moved his knight to counter Lucy's.

"Don't get picky with the small victories. It's good that you want to succeed, but you shouldn't be disappointed if you get something slightly less," Lucy replied, moving her bishop.

The game continued in silence, apart from the occasional curse from Tom as he overlooked a piece and lost his queen or rooks.

"Checkmate." Lucy had captured all of Tom's pieces, and finally cornered his king, winning the game.

A voice shouted out. "Tom! Lucy! Dinner's ready!"

"Cheer up, Tom. Tomorrow's another day." Lucy smiled. "Come

on. We can't keep Mum waiting."

*

Later that evening, Tom was sitting in a swivel chair in his room. He was surfing the internet, looking for chess moves. As he was looking at a gambit, he noticed a notification.

"rookieRook is online."

That was Alex, Tom's best and chess-obsessed friend, who was also going to the tournament. His Skype username was 'rookieRook'. Tom ignored him and kept scrolling down the webpage, burying himself in the complicated setups.

'rookieRook: Hi Tom'

'rookieRook: You on?'

'rookieRook: Your Skype tag says your online. Stop ingoring me'

'rookieRook: *ignoring'

Tom decided to answer him.

'kingOfPawns: WHAT?'

'rookieRook: Finally'

'rookieRook: I've been trying to talk to you all afternoon'

'kingOfPawns: I've been training'

'kingOfPawns: You know, for that big national chess tournament that is coming up in 2 weeks?'

'rookieRook: Oh lol sorry'

'kingOfPawns: It's ok :)'

'rookieRook: How'd you go?'

'kingOfPawns: Not the best. Sis beat me 21 times in 3 hours'

'rookieRook: Oh not good'

'kingOfPawns: Yeah. I have 2 weeks though. Hopefully I'll be ready :P'

'rookieRook: Ok'

'kingOfPawns: Ok, I'm gonna go look at more chess setups'

'rookieRook: Ok see you tomorrow'

'rookieRook is offline.'

Tom sighed, and went back to the webpages. He came across an interesting one, and grinned.

"Lights out, champ." His dad was leaning in the doorway.

"What? But it's only …" He checked his clock. It was 9:55 pm. He stopped himself. He might be learning new chess moves that could possibly win the tournament, but it was a school night. "Ok, Dad."

"How'd you go, anyway? Did you find anything?" Dad asked.

"Yeah, I found a few really good moves. Definitely going to try them," Tom replied.

"Nice. Make them count."

"Are you coming to the tournament?" Tom asked.

"Of course! I wouldn't miss it."

"What about Mum?"

"Erm …"

"What? Can't she come?" Tom had a sinking feeling in his stomach.

"She's really busy. The hospital's making her do extra hours so she won't be able to see you play. I'm really sorry, Tom," Dad said.

Tom was crestfallen. He was looking forward to having his entire family see him succeed. They'd be so proud of him. Now, it was just Dad. Tom knew Lucy would help Mum at work.

He wouldn't get to show both his parents what he was made of.

*

The weeks went by in a blur. Every day he'd play game after game with Lucy, always losing, never focusing. All he could think of was the tournament, which nobody would be there for. Even at school, people noticed that Tom was becoming a lot more introverted. Alex was the only one who cared, however. At lunch, he spotted Tom sitting on a bench by himself, and ran over to him.

"Hey, what's wrong?" Alex asked.

"Nothing," Tom replied. His voice was blank and flat.

"Don't give me that. I'm not stupid. I know there's something wrong," Alex snapped. "Just tell me. I'm here to help you." His tone went soft again.

"Ok, ok!" Tom exclaimed. "Mum and Lucy won't be able to make it to the chess tournament."

"T-that's it?" Alex look baffled.

Tom shrugged. "Yeah."

"So, why are you sitting around and moping? It's not that big a deal. Your dad's still coming, right?"

"Yeah, but you don't understand," Tom replied.

"What don't I understand?! It's not the end of the flipping world."

"The chess tournament was going to be the first time where my whole family would be there to see me succeed. I doubt that opportunity will come again." Tom sighed.

"Well, you won't succeed with this attitude. You still have to try."

"Oh, not this again," Tom muttered.

"You can still try your best, and even if you don't win, you'll still win!" Alex was standing on the bench now, trying to make a point. "You'll win by making someone proud! You'll succeed by proving that you can try!"

"How? No one will be there to be proud of me," Tom replied.

"Your dad's there! I'm going too! Your mum and sister will still be proud even if they're not there!" Alex was pumping his fist in the air, making a motivational speech.

"Yeah, I guess you're right."

"I am."

*

The tournament came a few days later, and Tom was extremely

9

nervous. The hall was crammed with all sorts of people. Alex, however, was literally white as a ghost.

"You okay, man?" Tom asked.

"Yeah, just nerves," Alex replied.

The games started, and Tom felt far too good for his competition. Each game ended in just a few minutes, Tom winning each one. He didn't have to try.

"Checkmate."

The girl he just beat groaned.

A voice boomed over the loudspeaker. "Players number 1 and number 43, make your way to the centre table for the final match."

Tom got even more nervous, and walked to the table. A tall, well-dressed kid was just sitting down. Tom sat down nervously. The kid grinned.

"Begin."

The game didn't last long. Twenty moves in and Tom had lost most of his pieces. He straggled around the board, but eventually lost.

"Hard luck." The kid grinned. "Good game."

They shook hands. At least the other kid did. Tom just flopped his hand like a limp noodle.

He lost, but his heart swelled when he saw Lucy and Mum arrive.

When the awards were handed out, the top three were asked to stand on the podium. As he looked over to his family and Alex from the podium, he knew he had truly won.

HELENA ANDREWS

The Mouldy Mattress Advantage

I am smart. I know it. You're not supposed to say it, but I am.

"Girls like us, all we've got are our smarts, Abby, you see?" This motto was hallowed.

It didn't matter when the mattresses started to go mouldy around the edges, and it didn't matter that the power got cut off last week. What mattered was that my mother had raised a smart little girl who was gonna do great things. Things greater than her and her mouldy mattresses. I'm six years old, and someday I'll be a lawyer, maybe even the prime minister. Those are things smart kids can do, you see.

*

I know it's an awful thing to say, but my mother isn't a smart woman. She doesn't even drive a car, or answer the angry red letters on the coffee table. Mum's lipstick bleeds into her wrinkles, because lip liner is too expensive. It's okay though, because she says that books are the best makeup a woman can wear anyway. I'm twelve years old. I want to help people someday.

*

I won $20 on a scratch ticket on Wednesday. I am sixteen today, and, because it's my lucky day and all, Mum said she'd treat me. "Everyone's a winner eventually," she told me. But I don't think so: not her, at least. Mum has something wrong with her bones. I used the $20 to buy her flowers and catch the bus to the hospital. I miss school sometimes, but that doesn't mean I'm not smart. I'm still smart.

*

I don't miss her as much anymore: not as much as I thought I would. I work hard, and I know I'm worth more than minimum wage. But they always say that there are better eighteen-year-olds than me – eighteen-year-olds who finished High School. The mattresses are mouldy, and the power got cut off last week. I know that someday I'll be a lawyer, maybe even the prime minister. Those are things a smart kid can do, you see. Because I am smart. I know it.

I know it.

STELLA JEAN STEVENS

I am Waiting for You

I am waiting for you.
In the shadow of the maunga
I am perched on the edge of the forest,
on the branch of the mighty kauri tree.
I slowly slide down the trunk and
hide amongst the ferns.
I see their silver underbellies glistening in the moonlight.
They bow their leaves to me in the wind as I slink past an
aging kauri snail.
Its meat is of no interest to me so I continue bashing through
the undergrowth.

What do you think of me?
I have a dark glossy coat that ripples in the breeze.
I am sly with a hooked tail,
like the curve of a koru.

I strip the trees of their growth.
I scramble, I scamper, I slink through the darkness.
I steal tree's life.
I destroy Mother Nature.

Do you hear me as I shake branches?
Do you hear me crunching on the leaves of the rimu?
Do you hear my victory screech,
my grunts as I climb to the canopy?
My hiss to scare you off.

But some don't hear my warning cry.
Some venture on in search of my blood.

I creep through the black,
across the gravel path.
Two blinding lights appear
from around the corner.
I freeze …

The lights stare at me.
I stare back with wide inky eyes.
I hear the sound of a gun.
I run.
I am darting through the bushes.
Swerving.
Scampering
I flee until I reach the safety
of my kauri tree.

I am waiting for you.
To give up …

I have survived the hunt.
I have dodged death.
I am still alive.
The fight has been fought.
The victory has been won.
I am curled up in my tree
waiting for your return.

My place is to taunt you
and destroy your mighty forest.

EMMA UREN

Once Upon a Time

When I was a child the world
was full of magic.
A twinkling cauldron, and I was the only one who knew
how to dance to its tune.
Experiences floated around me – they blur now in my
memory
until I am half-unsure what is a dream
and what is real.

When I was a child the fridge magnets were my friends
but I never realised how dull the colours were.
I went to school, and somehow, while I was away …
my world spun by in the fading light.

Now the planet is moving at a gigabyte rate
an exponential reaching for the heavens.
But every minute I spend typing
each rollercoaster exam
becomes a strict ritual in preparation for some grand
ceremony that never comes …
I am fortunate that
I fit the mould
our ancestors cast.
But even the swiftest feet can get tired sometimes
and even the strongest branches can break.

It is only when I pause
and look back over my shoulder
to see how far I have come
that I realise I can't even see the start line.

I am adrift in an ocean
of possibility.
Despite its brilliance, our expanding universe
makes me shiver
in the icy heart of the Milky Way.

They used to tell us
that everyone's a winner
and school is just for fun.
Why wouldn't it be when grades are a far-off shore?
Now we compete to be the best:
Our journeys have become a race
and I know
that everything can change upon the whim of the wind.

It's strange, but sometimes I long for
how the world used to be.

Operation X

"AGAIN!" the instructor yelled.

I slowly picked myself off the ground, wiping away the blood that was dripping from my lip. That was the third time I had been taken down, and it was only my first day.

Great work, Grey, I thought.

I wasn't used to this 'dancing about when you're fighting' that they were trying to teach us. After all the fights I had been in – and there had been a lot of street fights – I knew you fought dirty or you ended up with a broken face.

My opponent was built like a tank, with a face like a pile of bricks. Watt, I think, or at least that was what the others from his squad chanted when he smacked me around like a puppet. I took my place in the middle of the mat and raised my fists. Watt (the destroyer) did the same. His fists were about the same size as my head.

"How is this fair again?" I mumbled as our instructor shouted to start.

Five minutes later I was slumped against a wall, holding an ice pack to my face. My vision was still blurry, after I lost consciousness that last time.

I heard grunts and yells of pain, as the rest of Watt's squad totally annihilated one after the other of my own. It was hardly even. Where they had monsters and beasts, we had nerds and shrimps.

I winced as Watt smacked down Darwin, a lanky redhead with round spectacles and limbs that seemed too long for him to handle. As soon as I had boarded 'Invicta', the best ship in the Government Forces, I was chucked into Squad X, or 'experimentally placed' to see how I dealt with 'being with the underdogs ', as they put it. They certainly got the underdogs part right.

My thoughts were interrupted by the siren going off, signalling the end of combat training for the day. I breathed a sigh of relief and stayed where I was, as my squad made their way towards me, all of them battered and bruised from the beatings they had just received.

"You guys did well," I said, trying to sound supportive.

Hawk just nodded for all of them and leaned against the wall himself.

*

"How was your first combat training?" EDE asked. He was a short guy with jet-black hair and quite a temper when you pronounced his name E-D-E instead of E-Dee.

"Well, besides being pummelled by a guy twice my size, just fantastic," I replied.

They all chuckled a little, but were too sore to offer a greater response.

"We should get you to the healthcare bots," Hawk said, bending down and helping me up.

"Dude, we all need a trip to the healthcare bots," EDE replied dryly.

"Damn right you do." Watt and his squad were standing in front of us, not looking like they were ready to leave in a hurry.

Oh great, I thought, exactly what we need.

"Get lost, Watt!" Hawk said.

"Ah, get lost?" Watt said, raising an eyebrow and pushing Hawk back against the wall. His whole squad circled ours, six against four. Man, they loved making things even around here.

I quickly stepped in front of Hawk as Watt took a pace forward.

"Yeah. He said, 'Get lost.' Or are you too stupid to understand that concept?" I said, pulling myself as tall as I could at five foot nothing.

I had clearly caught him by surprise, so I took the opportunity, shoving all my body weight forward. I pushed him to the ground and started hitting him with my fists, over and over again, dodging out of the way every time he tried to punch back. But he quickly got over his surprise, and shoved me off and got to his feet. I leapt up and we circled each other.

I was dimly aware of the boys fighting the rest of Watt's squad, but from the sound of things, it wasn't going well.

No. Focus! Think. I tried to weigh the options. We can't beat them in a fight, that's obvious. But if we run ...

Then I had an idea. I slowly let Watt back me closer to the wall, but when he dove for me, I ducked out of the way, and he went head first into the wall. He dropped like a sack of concrete, and for a fearful moment I thought he was dead. But as soon as I saw him breathe, I was out of there. I ran before his squad could react, and thankfully the boys followed me. I heard shouts coming from the training room, but I didn't care. We just kept running along the long metal corridors of the spaceship.

*

I kept my head down during lunch, being careful not to draw attention to myself or the squad. If the rumours about Watt had travelled fast, then his squad would want revenge, and that wasn't something I was looking forward to.

"Grey? Grey!" EDE said punching my arm to get my attention.

"Ow!" I said. I had been hit enough for one day.

He nodded behind me, and I turned to find Rebecca, one of the girls from Watt's squad, standing there with a look of hatred on her face.

Before she could speak the crackling of the speaker system made us all stop.

"Squad X report to the command room immediately. Squad X report to the command room immediately."

The robotic speaker system echoed around the mess hall, causing the recruits to look up from their meals.

All units had finished training for the day.

Why would the commander want to talk to us? I wondered.

Everyone else seemed to be thinking the same thing as they started asking each other questions.

"What did they do now?"

"Probably blew something up."

"Yeah, or killed someone."

There was a sudden crash, and a body landed beside me.

It was Darwin. The boys heaved him to his feet, and I set his glasses straight. The room was still laughing. If this is what recruitment was like, then I wanted no part of it.

"Shut up," I shouted staring around the room in a death glare.

Somehow that did the trick and everyone silenced; maybe they had heard the Watt story, or some twisted version of it that made me seem even more intimidating. Either way worked for me.

I turned to Rebecca with a smile on my face and said, "If you stay away from us, I'll stay away from you. That way, everyone's a winner."

Then I walked out with my squad following, leaving a silent room behind us.

Learning to Win

"Jade! Hurry up. We'll be late for class."

I stuffed my tablet into my bag and grabbed a NutroBarr off the bench.

"Coming!" I called, racing towards the front door. My hi-board was lying haphazardly on the shelf where I had tossed it. Uh oh. I shook it, and it beeped angrily.

"Oh, sheesh, Trellin. I forgot to charge my board last night!"

"That doesn't matter. You can ride doubles with me. But hurry, please. You know how the burgs get when we're late …"

I climbed on beside her and held her waist. I hadn't ridden doubles for years – hopefully our combined weight wouldn't be too much for the board.

"We're getting our Third tests back today," Trellin said, as we zoomed down the street.

"Oh no. I hope I did okay."

"Jade, you always do fine. You're great at maths. There's nothing to worry about."

"I suppose," I replied. She was right, as usual. I had received A's for every test so far this year. But I couldn't shake the bubbling feeling in my stomach. Suppose I only got a B. Or even a C. It would mess up my chances for a good college next year.

Before I knew it, the apartments had flown by, and the School's grey gates loomed ahead. Trellin flew her hi-board right to our classroom door. We jumped off and opened the door cautiously, hoping the burg wouldn't notice.

"Trellin Page and Jade Gerstil. You are thirteen minutes late."

The burg's sickly-sweet, female voice drifted out from the classroom. That voice always seemed funny coming from its harsh metal exterior; a fact that had led to many cruel imitations from school students in the past. My great-grandpop said that the burgs reminded him of something called 'Daleks' from an old TV show. He had never liked them. Most older folk didn't. But, some oldies still wrote on paper, their aversion to technology was so great.

"I'm sorry, Seven …" Trellin began.

"Here at the School, we believe that punctuality is a very important skill for students to learn in order to become successful. Therefore, we cannot take lateness lightly. You have each gained one strike. Please refrain from lateness in the future, or we may be forced to put it on your record."

We both nodded meekly. It was useless to argue with a burg.

"Please take your seats. You may choose an activity to begin."

I walked to a free booth in the corner of the room and opened my interface. I selected a practice paper to work on.

A chat box opened up on the corner of my screen next to Seven's help program. It was Trellin.

'Burgs are sooo mean!' she had written. A crying face emoji popped up.

'I know!' I wrote in reply. 'I can't believe we got striked!'

I noticed Seven rolling towards me out of the corner of my eye, and quickly closed the window. I sighed. How could I concentrate on my work on a day like today? We would receive our test results in just fifty-four minutes. But the time ticked past at a speed that would embarrass a sloth.

*

When we were finally let out to go to maths class (after 'the ideal length of time for learning ', as Seven referred to it), my stomach was getting agitated. I was in two minds about the tests: I wanted the results, and at the same time I really didn't. It would be so embarrassing if I wasn't in the top two quartiles!

The test result list was already projected onto the wall when we walked into the classroom. Nineteen, our teaching burg, instructed us to check our scores.

I could barely breathe. I didn't look at the list. A hundred worried voices clouded my brain. What if …? What if …?

"Jade! I told you there was nothing to worry about!"

I raised my head to see Trellin's beaming face. Well, if she was smiling, I can't have done too badly.

I checked the list and my mouth fell open. I was at the top!

But – how could that be? Maybe Nineteen had made an error in her calculations. There were plenty of people better than me in the class. I had never been in the top three before. Fourth, sure, but not first. Mayzelia was the girl who usually came on top.

Still, I wasn't complaining. It was like a dream come true. I knew it was bad of me, but I felt a secret happiness at beating everyone.

I scanned the rest of the list. Trellin had come fifth, an excellent mark. I turned to her.

"Good job!" I whispered, enfolding her in a hug.

"Look, Jade. Mayzelia came last."

I looked up at the list again, surprised. Trellin was right. What had happened? How could someone drop from first to last? Maybe Mayzelia was sick.

I looked over at Mayzelia. Her face was stony. Poor Mayzelia. I didn't know what I would do if I failed a test.

"Please begin your work," Nineteen said. "I will be coming to each of you for individual feedback." She began with Mayzelia.

Everyone in the class ducked their head, but I could tell twenty-nine pairs of ears were straining to hear Mayzelia and Nineteen.

"Mayzelia, you have failed Test Number 3. Your average has now dropped to 89%."

I heard Mayzelia take a deep breath. "Well, maybe I want to

make mistakes sometimes. Maybe I want to actually learn. Not just win all the time." Her voice shook.

Nineteen hummed frantically. This was an unexpected situation.

"Here at the School, we believe that everyone's a winner," she began, her polite voice unfazed.

"Really?" Mayzelia cut in. "What are we really gaining by winning?"

Nineteen's humming grew louder, like a swarm of angry bees.

Oh, Mayzelia. Just be quiet, I pleaded silently.

"Here at the School, we believe that respect for others is a vital skill for –"

"What about telling the truth? Because your system's stupid. We're overworked and over-assessed, and for what? For the best jobs? So we can go on being slaves to our work our whole lives?"

There was silence for a few seconds. Then Nineteen beeped.

"Mayzelia Verim. Please report to the principal's office."

*

Mayzelia didn't come back to class that day. Nor was she at the School for the rest of the week. Rumours circulated our class, but no one had the courage to ask a burg where she had gone. Months flew by, and soon everyone had forgotten about her.

It was only on a cold, grey mid-winter evening, when I had stayed late at the School, that I suddenly remembered about Mayzelia. A burg stood silent at the front of the deserted classroom.

Surely there would be no harm in asking.

"Excuse me … There was a girl here, earlier in the year … Her name was Mayzelia Verim. I was just wondering what happened to her?"

The burg turned slowly to look at me. Its unmoving steel eyes looked faintly sinister in the shadows.

"Here at the School, we believe that everyone's a winner …"

DHRUTI JAYNA RAMANLAL

Free of Peace

It doesn't talk.

It stalks every step, haunts every night, stares at every tear, divides the soul with fear and doubt. A Grim Reaper who's forgotten his blimmin' job.

The others can't see it. Standing behind me, freezing all warm red roads. Not a friend or enemy knows. Why would they? They smile and laugh with the sun. They sing melodies and fly with the breeze. They let the wind run through their feathers and, when the day is over, they return to their warm nests and do it all again tomorrow. They're all winners.

*

One day I was walking home, the world crying with me. My shoelace untied and everything inside me screamed, the wind wailed, the rain begged me not to stop. To keep going.

I couldn't though. I had to stop and tie my lace and I never felt so afraid.

I could feel it coming closer. I could feel it reaching out to my backpack. I – I ran.

*

Some days I would cry myself to sleep, and some days I would replay a certain memory over and over again. I forced myself to. Some days I would dream about running far away, and some days I would draw on myself in the bathroom. The drawings were jagged at first like ugly scars, but now patterns are forming. Round and lovely like henna. I needed bandages for each one.

Can you imagine how it feels? When someone is talking directly to you but is actually just talking to a walking corpse? Feeling like someone else is pulling the strings and using your own tongue to say whatever they want?

There are voices in my head, shrill and scratchy. I can't make their screams stop. They never stop.

I have to end this.

End having to feel like I'm drenched in an indomitable rot. End this addiction to destroying myself: the voices, the screaming, the dissociation, the shadow.

Everything had to end. Everything.

*

I suppose that's why I'm on this cliff, looking at the sea and the rocks. The sun is dying before me.

I have been here the whole afternoon, getting closer to the edge by the hour.

I can do this. I will do this.

Something feels wrong. It feels like the grass has tiny hands with a firm grip on my shoes. The wind is pushing against me with all its might. The sea is rushing in and preparing to cushion my fall and the rocks try to sink.

I won't let this stop me. I fight forward against the wind and now I am at the very edge.

The sun is halfway gone when I hear that voice: warm and sweet. It can't be mine. Mine is hoarse and cold. But it sounds so similar to mine.

"You don't have to do this."

"Of course I do. It's the only way," I whisper.

"To end your suffering? Sure it feels like that, but –"

"I don't care!" I interrupt.

"What about the people who do care? What about them?"

"No one cares!"

"How do you know? Tell me, how do you know? You haven't spoken to anyone. Not your family who know nothing; not your friends that you walk home with most days; not your teachers; not anyone!"

"So?"

"So, how can anyone help you?"

"Okay, and this is you helping me? Screaming at me with questions that you already know the answers to?"

"I'm giving you a choice. You just need to be brave enough to take it."

"I don't think I can do that," I beg.

"Sure you can. You just gotta take a leap of faith."

I stare back at the sun and watch as the last drop of light vanishes into the sea.

I have made my decision.

With my shoulders back and a deep breath, I take a last glance at the evening sky. A small glimmer of light is all I need.

I head home, admiring the birds, the smell of freshly barbecued meats and the opening lines of *The Spanish Sahara*. I realize it is the first time in a long time I feel like I have won a gold medal: like I have achieved something that only I know about. It is a very good feeling. Don't get me wrong, my shadow is still following me, but I guess I am okay with that.

*

I was so caught up in my own achievement that I almost didn't see her. I nearly walked right into her as she sat there, alone, in the middle of the footpath.

She was crying.

I contemplated for a second what had happened on the cliff, what I had been through. The shadow met my gaze with a silent question.

I answered by mustering up the courage to ask, "Are you okay?"

AUDREY VITERO

Cloud Your Integrity

In a small town in the middle of the forest lived a sick man, who knew his day was near. The man was known for his fortune and owned a vast amount of land. Without anyone to pass it on to, he decided that one of the good people of this town might put it to good use. With this in mind, he sent his men to spread the word about his condition.

Word travelled fast in this small village. Everyone was interested in owning the old man's wealth; greedy or not, everyone knew about the big news. But how would the man choose his successor?

"I will give each one of the eligible citizens a seed. Plant it and take care of it, for owning farmland means having a knowledge of gardening. This will determine who will own my riches."

The crowd that had gathered in the old man's house was taken aback by his announcement, for even though planting was what most families did for a living, not everyone had the knowledge of how to do it. But since the reward would surely be astounding, the people reluctantly agreed. Each citizen was given a seed, and they all went rushing back to their houses, keen to be the first to grow it.

One member of the crowd that day was Emil. He casually accepted a seed.

Being a rich geezer would be nice, he thought.

It would mean he wouldn't have to travel to that other town to sell goods, like the knitted bags his mum made. More importantly, it would mean his elderly grandparents not having to work anymore. Working always wore his grandpa out. Emil felt a rush.

"Ahh, I could really get used to that!" Emil smiled.

He went back home, greeting people along the way and wishing them luck with their seeds.

"Thank you, Emil. Perhaps you could make me some bags when I'm the richest girl in town?" Astrid teased, showing off her smile.

Emil had always liked Astrid. He liked the way she spoke with wit, how she was always quick on her feet, and especially how she could make Emil's heart skip a beat.

"I've told you, Astrid, I don't make them; I sell them," Emil replied.

"Yeah, alright. Reserve your best designs for me, eh?" she said, ignoring what he just said.

Walking into his house, Emil saw his mother knitting.

"Did you get a seed like everyone else?" she asked.

"Yes, Mum. We are going to be rich, I promise you that!" he exclaimed, really liking the idea of living in luxury.

*

A few days after he had planted the seed, it had still not grown: not even a sprout was coming out.

"You have to be patient," he told himself.

He hadn't heard about any of his neighbours' seeds either; they obviously didn't want anyone knowing about their plants.

But Emil was worried. Had he put too much water on it? Had he buried it way deeper than necessary? Surely that couldn't be: his grandpa had helped him, and nothing could have gone wrong.

Everyone seemed to have distanced themselves from one another, and he wondered why. Emil passed by Astrid's house and talked to her.

"Well, I guess neither of us stands a chance to get rich, huh?" she smiled thinly.

"Your seed won't grow either?" Emil asked, shocked that Astrid had the same problem.

"How should I know, Emil? My mother wouldn't even let me get the seed into a pot. Says it's nothing but nonsense," Astrid complained.

"Sorry to hear that." He really was.

On the way back home, Emil thought about what he could do with his plant. Should he put some manure on it? No, that would be cheating.

He continued taking care of the pot for a few more days. It was exactly five days from now until the old man's deadline.

Little did young Emil know – little did anyone in the town know – that the old man had set a test of the people's honesty and conscience. He was about to find out who was who!

*

When the day arrives, Emil is reluctant to bring his petty pot to the old man's house. With the cold breeze of March contrasting with the hot sun, he walks to the gathering on the flat land at the centre of town. He sees a sea of potted plants with beautiful and pompous colours, their beauty putting him in a slight trance. Everyone is boasting about their own pretty plants, making Emil feel wretched.

People begin to notice his plantless pot. A woman laughs, drawing more attention from others. People snicker and whisper. He is about to run away, when the old man walks out of his house with his cane.

Everyone falls silent. Emil feels the tension, the air growing heavier. Why is he bothered? It's not like he has any chance of winning.

The old man scans the crowd and the sea of plants. He sees Emil's pot, then meets Emil's eye, and smiles. "My friends, what beautiful plants you have. I have chosen my successor."

"Who is it? Tell us now," a man carrying a plant with purple and green leaves cries.

"Before that, I would like to tell you that all the seed I've given you was boiled."

Everyone is baffled.

"That is why it did not grow!" the old man exclaims, smiling widely. "Everyone except Emil has obviously swapped a different seed for the one they were given. And the truth is, you were all given the same type of seed, yet you have returned with all manner of different plants in your hands."

He turns to Emil. "Come, child. I declare you as my successor. Use my means well."

The old man invites Emil over, and all eyes are on him. Only a minute ago they were all laughing about his pot. Now he is declared as the heir to a fortune.

Emil stands by the old man, his legs trembling. "I ..." His voice falters.

Before he can say anything, the old man speaks. "Do what is right, not what is easy. Do not let gold cloud your integrity." There is determination in his voice.

Emil thinks about what the old man has said for a second. He knows everyone in this town well; he knows they didn't mean to cheat. The people in this town are just tired of the struggles of being poor.

"Now, what were you saying, young man?" The old man turns to him and smiles again.

Emil is now rich. It hasn't sunk in yet. Emil knows he wants the money, the riches, everything. But does he need it all?

"I – uh – I would like to divide the land that I now own between every one of you to take care of. I know that you didn't mean to cheat, and I forgive you," he says, earning smiles from the people around him.

The old man pats Emil's shoulder. "I like that," he says quietly. "Everyone's a winner."

VICTORIA SUN

I Am Pluto

There was a lengthy war in regard to the Sun,
Some wanted to be close while some did not,
But once everybody got their lot,
The damage could not be undealt.

With each ray that was diminished
The war inched closer to insanity.
Slowly they lost their humanity,
And eventually I was banished.

I was not like Mercury.
Mercury who fought with such rage,
Wrath of the calibre that does not wither with age,
Mercury who possessively guards first place.

I was not like Venus.
Venus who enchanted with an iridescent glow,
Luminescence far more entrancing than any sight men know,
Venus glows contently in second place.

I was not like Earth.
Earth, who did not hold lightly billions of lives,
Minds that could end with the cold embrace of knives,
Earth who deems third place adequate.

I was not like Mars.
Mars, who was constantly capricious,
Icy, then stormy, but always judicious,
Mars who wanders to fourth.

I was not like Jupiter.
Jupiter who was a gentle giant,
Colossal, yet ever so compliant,
Jupiter who settles wherever it drifts to be.

I was not like Saturn.
Saturn, who did not yearn for the Sun,
As for many chunks of ice and dust, Saturn is the one,
Saturn does not admire since it is admired.

I was not like Uranus.
Uranus, who unyieldingly sought seclusion,
Denial in an unforgiving and bitter fusion,
Uranus who holds a timeless grudge.

I was not like Neptune.
Neptune, who fought an internal war,
One that shook it to its very core.
Neptune who learns how to conquer itself.

I am Pluto.
Pluto who listened to its heart,
Who in the war played no part,
Pluto who hurts no one.

Pluto who is a planet not.

Just for Mum

All you want to do is make her proud,
Because she's your number one fan in the crowd.
She's the one who got you here,
And now disappointing her is your biggest fear.

But mother won't worry,
She'll say there's no need to be sorry.
Because she will love you no matter what.
Will she be ashamed? No she will not.

As long as you did the best you could
And that you are sure that you did good.
Then that's all she cares about,
Because she loves you throughout.

She'll come in with arms widely spread
To give you a hug and a kiss on the head.
Because in her eyes
You will always be
A winner!

MELISSA BLACKETT

Dancing in the Dusk Sunlight

Dancing in the dusk sunlight on top of Primrose Hill,
I see the houses light up one by one.
The tankers roll in over the bridge
Getting to the farms just before nightfall is upon.
I can hear the trickling water of Ohinemuri River,
I close my eyes and inhale the smells
That linger through the air,
Being carried by the breeze
Fish n Chips down at the Burger bar,
The BBQ cooking meat.
I close my eyes and embrace all the sounds,
Laughter symbolising happy moments being shared
Between whanau and friends.
Car horns tooting at each other
Saying Hello with a wave of the hand.
Hanging out the window,
I feel the connection between
The community down below.
The breeze is no longer.
The tankers have gone.
The laughter in the breeze now no longer,
As I dance in the dusk sunlight on top of Primrose Hill.

Lady Liberties in a Line

Nobody really knew when Larry Underwood and his sideshow first appeared at the Mayholm County Fair. The man was as seamlessly knitted into the fabric of our community as the workmen who lounged in the Plaza, or the matronly croon of our local choir every Sunday afternoon.

There was something special about Larry and his stall, a thread of mystery which transformed the field at Mayholm County School into a forum for daring feats and elusive victory, and reeled in a gathering of enthralled children every Saturday, without fail.

The stall was a thing of wonder. A simple construction – front counter and backboard, supported by four poles with a tarpaulin draped over – it overflowed with intense colour. Meccado racing cars were stacked elegantly on one tiered pole; another was layered with stuffed bears which could fill a small house. Rows of crushed cotton candy, folded into shiny plastic sleeves lined the back wall, releasing the enticing smell of sugar, which wafted in tendrils across the neighbouring storefronts and out through the fairground.

To us, there was nothing – nothing – that quite paralleled the effervescent energy of this place.

On the centre of the counter, fringed by jumping-jacks and thumb traps with lavish designs, rested a large box. A huge brass sign affixed to the front christened the contraption 'Underwood's Luck Machine', and declared, 'Everyone A Winner! A Dollar Per Dial!' More than anything, we were hooked on the sheer simplicity of that tagline – one Lady Liberty was all it cost to take home a piece of the Playground of Eden.

Entry into the ranks of pocket-salary earners qualified you to take part in the high point of Mayholm County life. On a week-to-week basis we'd line up, clutching our silver dollars. Our parents always stepped back into spectatorship: this was our sovereign ritual. One by one we'd file forward. Larry Underwood, sporting red suspenders and a jovial yellow shirt with frilled cuffs, maintained a theatrical air, which added to the spectacle.

Once the coin was inserted, the machine would print a ticket, and with a wordless flamboyance, our thespian would retrieve and present the slip to the eager buyer. The process was supposed to entitle the winner to a prize from the store. In retrospect, we never seemed to see anything won. This was part of the magic. The ticket always read something indecipherable and important, shrouded in mystery, which begged to be folded up and tucked in the pocket of your Saturday dungarees. Amidst all the litter washed up after the fair, you never found a stray message from the Luck Machine.

In the schoolyard, we passed stories of curios beyond our wildest dreams, attainable only at the behest of Underwood's Luck Machine.

The machine, we agreed, had an aloof disposition. The mystery of the thing – and the hilarious consternation written on our mothers' faces – kept us coming back, as if we were attached to a spring. Every weekend. Larry Underwood was the silent gatekeeper to the most engrossing element of Mayholm County life.

*

One Saturday, as per usual, all the boys from our neighbourhood stood in a loose queue in front of Underwood's stall. I stood shoulder-to-shoulder with my cousin, who, with my aunt, was up visiting from a county several hours' drive away.

Everyone was fussing, acting in a slightly over-dramatic manner; we thrummed with anticipation, eager to show a newcomer our small-town attraction, the gem of the fair. Quietly, I think we all hoped my cousin would be the one to win a prize and deliver us all a scoop of first-hand news to disperse in classes when school started the next week.

I maintained a cool air at my cousin's side, his quiet sidekick distant from the excited blathering of my friends. I peered around, and my gaze happened upon my aunt, who stood several yards away with my mother. I was startled.

The kids of the school revelled in the uniform pinched-anxious-prudent pout that our assembled parents adopted every week. The parents were outsiders, and outsiders were essential to the sanctity of any worthwhile ritual. What I registered on my aunt's face, however, wasn't misunderstanding. It was rage. I knew anger; I knew the frustrated wrath of my friends' parents and mine, but it took several years before I came to recognise the cold, hard hatred that my aunt directed with a piercing focus, straight at Larry Underwood.

My aunt noticed me then, and her expression softened into familiarity before she shifted her eyes to the machine on the stall counter. I watched as she scanned the brass plaque – "Underwood's Luck Machine: Everyone A Winner!" – and the grotesque look returned to her face.

Disquieted, I turned back to my cousin, who craned to watch as a girl in a pinstriped blouse received her note, cast a doleful look at a sky-blue monkey hanging from the front crossbar, and pocketed the message. She joined the others who had had their turn, and now waited wide-eyed for the rest of us.

We meandered forward. I won a wolf-whistling contest with a classmate, and my cousin seemed pleased. When we finally reached our turn, I inserted my coin into the slot and noticed something off about Larry Underwood. His jowls, usually as stoic and unmovable as our resolve to return, quivered. His tongue darted out to lick his lips in a rather lizard-like manner, and I could swear his hand shook as he retrieved my note. What it read, I can't for the life of me remember, because at that moment my cousin stepped forward, and Larry Underwood took a step back.

All eyes, affixed to Underwood's machine, now flicked to the man himself. Underwood never moved from behind his machine. It was an unspoken rule, a constant of the lore surrounding the spectacle. Underwood vanished during the week; nobody ever saw him set up or pack down. But for a precious few hours, he was as present as a town monument, on the school field, in his stall, behind his machine.

Now, like a tree uprooted, Underwood gathered momentum. One staggered step careered into three more. All the while, Underwood's eyes darted between my cousin, and my aunt. Then the man collapsed.

I didn't understand, then. I do now. The whole debacle, the emergency doctor who came to visit, the policemen who held each of our Lady Liberties to glint in the sun before placing them in a transparent bag, made for great stories in the schoolyard.

Our aunt asked about Underwood on her next visit up. She smiled when I told her we hadn't seen him since.

JOANNA LI

How to Fix a Broken Heart

Start small. So you've spent days, weeks, months, even years feeling like the Titanic right before she sank. If you want to stop, but you begin each day by staring at the ceiling – is it worth it to get up? – then you start small. You're not going to suddenly bounce up and go frolicking through the meadows and sunsets, and sunsets over meadows.

Know that you're doing just fine. That's it. Just know. Whether you spent the day blasting out music until the bass hurt your ears and your soul, or you ate dumplings until the hurt in your stomach matched the hurt in your heart, until the stomach in your brain was satisfied. You did just fine. Know that you're okay, that you got through yesterday, you got through today, and you'll get through tomorrow.

Secondly. At the end of every day. Turn off the lights. Lie on your bed. Close your eyes. Listen to the silence. Listen to your breathing. In, out, in, out.

*

This is how I began.

A man is staring into the window of a closed restaurant, dark and dusty with stools overturned onto the tables. His coat billows out in the night air, thick and soft – cashmere probably. He looks far too wealthy to be wandering the side streets at this time of night, but then again, what do we know? The people bustle around him, taking no notice of the way he stands, or the slant of his shoulders. Or maybe they do notice: they notice too much. Yet the soft murmur of idle small talk is even quieter than silence, and a thousand times more timid. Have they learned yet that the greatest disservice is to look away?

When I try to imagine pain, this is what I see.

*

We study the Islamic revolution in class, and I am reminded of the horror in the world, the blood on our hands. I get angry on behalf of someone else, and it feels good. Not right, but good. It feels good to be feeling something, even if that feeling is anger. They always say anger is red, but I think that anger is black, all consuming, and biting from the inside.

I know this is a danger, that the blackness can harden into something ugly, can be twisted and cruel.

*

The morning after, I clog the plughole by cutting my hair in the kitchen sink. Watching it all swirl down the drain feels important, like the way my new choppy fringe feels important.

And I head out.

The smell of coffee grounds and sweet jazz is the perfect background for a café courtship. I could laugh, watching this young, baby faced boy with a bun and stubble. He would be smooth, if he isn't so blindingly happy. But really, who needs smooth when you're happy?

The girl's smiling indulgently at him. She's careful: smart girl. Too long working behind the till and in front of tables has taught her to be cautious. A pretty waitress with a pretty face. Would this boy know any better?

He stays long after his coffee cup is drained, and then some, and I hide my smile behind my napkin when he gets another to go. The girl watches the door swinging after him, wistfully. She wants to leave with him, I can tell, but loyalty to her apartment rent, and tonight's dinner makes her stay.

What happens next? I don't know. I finish my bagel, and I leave through the glass door, into the rain. Is he a regular? Will he become one? It's not for me to decide, and I will not meddle, because they deserve that at least. Like they deserve everything else. Like they deserve the world.

*

Picture this: there's a girl sitting on the curb. Her dress is glittery and her hair is straight. A black duffel bag sits by her feet. She's waiting for someone, something; you can tell in the way she checks her phone, the constant flipping of blonde hair over slim shoulders. It's very easy to believe she's irritated at a late parent, but there's always the little voice insisting she's been stood up, she was supposed to have a beautiful night with a beautiful boy but now she's alone and cold on the roadside. And isn't that the greatest tragedy of all, the universe of anticipation and excitement for the night ahead, wasted on someone who ended up bailing. So quickly that universe can swallow itself, bitter, sickly and grey until it's ugly and twisted. The watcher feels pity and anger and sympathy towards her all at once, in the single second they spare her a glance. Does she deserve better?

Doesn't everybody?

And I learn to see hope in love again. Because that girl is still hopeful, still oh so hopeful. Yes, maybe she is naïve, but she is young, and there is hope in the tomorrows, there is hope in new beginnings. This is what you must do, this is what we all must do.

*

Now imagine the front yard of a dirty house, a family spread out. Two lounging on the steps, one leaning out of the window, three sitting on the grass. A baby wanders back and forth between two flowered pot plants, ignoring the cold in its nappy. The love is palpable in the air, and the sky is cloudy and grey, yet it's not hard to picture a lazy summer sun above the house. Maybe it would make the off-white paint flaking from the walls more natural,

42

cleaner. There's a simplicity that's so certain, so honest, it's palpable.

*

Finally, a snapshot: there's a couple leaving the supermarket. They're weighed down by the plastic bags of bread and milk and jam and carrots, but their heads and voices are light with laughter. It's hard to imagine anything bad can happen in a world where people can still laugh like that. Governments will fall, cities will burn, and the world will tear itself into ruin with war, yet that couple will keep on laughing and laughing and laughing, because it matters not what will happen tomorrow, but what happens now. This is what it means to be beautiful, to be happy, to be alive.

*

Picture this: me – happy, in soul and spirit. This is who I want to be.

And finally, know that you have won. You are the winner; we are all winners. Because we are here: we are here and breathing and alive. We are here today, and that's all that matters.

Madness

When I was 4 and my father left home, my mother told me that love was a dead man's game. She said, "If you fall in love, run away as fast as you can and don't look back."

When I was 8 and my eldest cousin ran away from home, my aunt told me that no one won in the game of love. She said, "Love won't hesitate to crush your heart like a mere scrap of paper, even if you spent your life making it."

When I was 12 and my year 7 teacher got divorced, the principal told us that playing love was even worse than gambling. He said, "The stakes are too high, and you end up selling your soul."

When I was 16 and my sister's boyfriend cheated on her, her best friend told me that fate had rigged the game of love so that no one won. She said, "It was a mirage, too good to last, too intoxicating to believe, yet too addictive to give up."

When I was 20 and my best friend got married, his widowed mother told me that she wished he'd never sold his soul to the devil called Love. She said, "It is a contract that drains your life source without you knowing."

Now I'm 24 and I met you, everyone told me that I'd end up bruised, battered, and bloodied. You said, "Love is madness. And anyone sane enough to play, will not survive; because love isn't about the ending. It's the memories that count. Everyone who plays the game of love, wins."

I Am Not

I am not,
Malala.
I have not sacrificed everything so that girls around the world
have opportunities to be educated,
But that does not mean that I do not have courage.
I can face my fears like a burning fire.

I am not,
Albert Einstein.
I have not discovered how the world works,
But that does not mean I am not smart.
Thoughts can flutter in my head like galaxies swirling around
the universe, and I can put them into place.

I am not,
Madonna.
I have not changed the world with my music,
But that does not mean I am not talented.
My songs can light up the sky, my humour can brighten the
darkest night.

I am not,
Anyone else.
But that does not mean I am not amazing,
That does not mean I cannot change the world.
I can,
Because I am, Me.

Zack's First Day

Mr Reynolds had been talking for about five minutes when the door flew open and in stomped another student. My god, he was handsome. His eyes scanned the classroom, finding the only empty seat next to me. He thumped down on the chair.

"You're new, ay? I'm Cory," he said offering his hand.

"Umm, Zack," I said grasping it.

We exchanged some small talk, then he asked if I played sport. I hesitated. I'd figured out by now that he was probably one of the star rugby players. Carved Maori muscles, athletic build, contrasting with my scruffy, sun-bleached, brown hair and ghostly skin. I was well toned and played rugby too, but compared to him I was like a skinny slab of meat.

"Yeah, I play."

"Cool! You should come to practice after school."

I wanted to say yes, but I knew that I would probably be the worst one there and they'd tell me to get on my bike. He could see how unsure I was and gave me a pat on the back.

"C'mon, mate, it'll be fun!" he encouraged.

"Okay," I relented.

Cory grinned. "Awesome! Three-thirty. Bottom field." He pointed out a few of his friends sitting a bit further up in the class: the rowdiest kids in the room, all rugby players too. I wasn't surprised.

When the bell rang, students scrambled out of the door, and I was left by myself to find my next class.

*

I'd found a spot under a tree to eat lunch. Apart from that first encounter with Cory, I'd not made any friends, and boy, I wasn't game enough to go sit with all the rugby players. This place was nice enough. My sandwich and apple had been devoured when a trio of kids came over to me.

"Hey," said the girl sitting down next to me.

"Hi?" I responded, unsure of what she was doing.

"Listen up. We heard you singing before and we want you to join the musical."

Oh damn. I'd had my earphones in and must have unwittingly started singing.

"Wait, who are you? Why do you want me?"

The girl flicked her lengths of dirty blonde hair. She had a pretty face – not really noticeable until you looked though. She extended her hand and took off her beanie with a cheeky grin.

"Bobbie," she said.

"Who, you?" I asked, uncertain of whether she was introducing her friends or herself.

"Yes me!" she sighed, and turned around to the other two. "Why does everyone say that?"

"I'm —"

"Shhh, buster," she said, cutting me off. "This is Reggie and Kalidas."

The two boys nodded at me.

"Well I'm —"

I was cut off again. Gosh this girl could be annoying.

"Zack. Yeah, I know."

I raised my eyebrows.

"It says on your backpack," Bobbie explained. "Anyway, we are low on numbers for this year's musical, and you've got a voice on you there, kid. You willing to help us out?"

I had never been in a musical before, but I wanted some friends, whether they were jocks or drama geeks.

"Fine."

"Fantastic! Rehearsal's at three-thirty in the auditorium. See ya!" Bobbie yelled, wandering off with her friends.

"But ..." Too late: she was already gone.

Great! I thought. *Now I have to choose, rugby or musical.*

*

At 3:30 that afternoon I was heading towards the bottom field. I'd decided that if I could impress these guys, I'd probably be protected and more respected than if I was in the musical. Guilt engulfed me about letting Bobbie down.

"ZAACCCKKK!"

I tried to put a smile on my face as Cory greeted me.

"This is my new bro, Zack," Cory said introducing me to the team.

"Kia ora, cuz!" said a boy who was twice the size of me.

Some people looked concerned at how tiny I was, but Cory kept hold of me until he'd finished naming everyone.

Training was manageable. We performed a few drills. I struggled to keep up. Everything was going fine until we started tactical movement. Apart from Cory, no one seemed to understand what they were doing. They didn't have any comprehension of how to interpret Cory's instructions.

I started to shine. I was understanding the commands, playing the ball right and telling the others what to do in a way they could follow. The other boys weren't dumb; they just didn't know how to execute Cory's commands.

Once things started to run smoother, Cory called for a break.

"Man, Zack! I've never seen things run that well before! Even though you're not the umm ..."

"Yeah, I know. I'm not the best in power or strength," I completed for him.

"But you sure know how to work a game!" Cory congratulated.

"Thanks!"

I looked at my phone. It read 4:15.

"Uh, Cory?" I said.

"Yeah?" he replied, turning around.

"I – gotta go – uh – home. Right now!" I said.

I grabbed my bag and ran off towards the school, cursing myself for not thinking up a better excuse. The musical rehearsal finished at 5:00, so I'd still have three quarters of an hour to make it up to Bobbie.

At the auditorium, I rushed into the bathroom to get changed. I came out and found my way backstage, where Bobbie was yelling at someone to 'Hurry up and get their lines right!'

"Um, excuse me?" I squeaked.

"Now you decide to show up, junior. What in the world were you doing anyway?" Bobbie snapped as she spun around.

"He was with me." Cory stepped out of the shadows to face Zack. "Care to explain yourself?"

I looked at the floor and put my hand over my nose. My voice was barely audible when I muttered, "I really wanted to fit in, and I didn't want you to think that I was a freak for being in the musical, and Bobbie, I didn't want you to think I was a stuck up rugby player who doesn't care about anyone's feelings, and I'm so sorry, and I'll just go now!"

I turned and started to leave, knowing I would never find friends now when I heard laughter coming from behind me.

"Zack, oh my gosh!" Bobbie managed through her chuckling. "What did you think? That the 'drama geeks' and the 'jocks' hated each other? We're not in the movies!"

"In fact, I'm one of the lead roles in the musical," Cory chuckled.

"But how do you attend both practices?" I asked, very confused.

"Bobbie was playing with ya. She knew you were coming to practice so she put the rehearsal on the same day."

"How did she know?" I asked, now very confused.

Cory bent down and kissed Bobbie on the lips.

"That's how," Bobbie giggled.

"Oh. Right." My cheeks turned bright red.

"Do you still want to be in this?" Bobbie asked. "And play rugby as well?"

"If you still want me. I've been an idiot!"

Bobbie laughed. "Yeah you have, but as I said, we're desperate."

"You'd be a real asset to the team," Cory said.

I gulped. "Okay."

Bobbie high-fived me. "Only, if there's no more assuming, then everyone's a winner!"

The Winning Wish

Jimmy was a loser.

Everything Jimmy entered, he came last.

He was last in cross country because he took a wrong turn and got lost. He was last in the swimming competition because when he dived in, his togs fell off. He even lost at marbles because he broke his thumb as he flicked his marble.

He was definitely a loser and all Jimmy wanted was to be a winner.

Jimmy was walking home after losing again, this time at arm wrestling, when suddenly something fell from the sky. It hit Jimmy on the head, knocking him down, and making him see stars. Jimmy got up off the ground groaning. When he looked up, what he saw nearly made him fall back down again in shock.

Floating before him was a man who looked like he had just wandered off the set of a movie about a really bad used-car salesman. He had balding hair, a leather jacket, and a cigar that looked like it hadn't been lit and was just there to make him look cooler. But his top half wasn't even the weirdest bit. From his waist down, there was a green mist that was connected to an old, rusty trophy.

Jimmy rubbed his eyes and looked at the man again. He looked strangely like a genie.

"Who are you?" Jimmy asked, bewildered.

"I am Boris; I am now your genie."

"Wow!" spluttered Jimmy. "So if I wished for anything it would come true?"

"You get three wishes," replied Boris.

Jimmy felt like he was going crazy, his mind racing with things that he wanted to wish for. But his mouth suddenly got the better of him. Out blurted, "I wish for a new pair of sports shoes!"

"Your first wish is granted," said Boris as he disappeared back into the trophy.

Suddenly a pair of non-branded pink and brown sports shoes appeared at Jimmy's feet. Jimmy sighed, picked up the trophy and the very ugly shoes, and started his long walk home.

When he got home, Jimmy rushed into his bedroom and put the trophy and the shoes on his desk. As he flopped onto his bed in exhaustion he heard a strange tapping noise coming from his desk. It got louder and louder, until it sounded like a very loud marching band with no sense of rhythm. Jimmy groaned and sat up, looking around for the source of the noise. His eyes landed on the trophy where he supposed Boris was inside, tapping away just to be a pain. He walked over to the trophy and gave it a slap. Out came Boris who was grinning from ear to ear.

"What?" asked Jimmy in an exasperated tone.

"It's awfully boring sitting in my trophy. You still have two wishes left," replied Boris.

Jimmy stared daggers at Boris. He didn't think much of the outcome of his last wish, but suddenly he had an epiphany.

"I know!" he said, his face lighting up. "I wish that I can be the winner at the next school running race."

"Huh," said Boris, who was slightly distracted snacking on a packet of potato chips. "It is done!" His voice was rather dramatic, whilst he spat out bits of chip.

The next morning, Jimmy woke up the happiest person ever. Racing from his bedroom, he checked his calendar. He did a little victory dance. Next week there was a huge running race that had the school's biggest trophy for the winner. What luck!

A week later, Jimmy was milling around the school field where the race was going to take place. Looking around, he saw the race commentators talking into fancy microphones. They walked over to a kid named Dan Walker. Dan won everything, and they were asking him if he felt good about the race. Jimmy smiled because he knew that Dan would not be winning today. Jimmy was going to win and, hopefully, by a lot.

The commentators called the participants up to the start line. Jimmy hoped that Boris had got it right. After all, he hadn't quite got the first wish correct. He heard his name called, and with his heart in his throat, he lined up next to Dan. Dan looked at Jimmy and smirked. People were looking at Jimmy and laughing because they knew he was a loser.

But this would be the day that changed all that: this would be the day he would become a winner. A BIG winner!

The starter stepped up and raised his air-horn. He started counting down, "Three, two, one!" He pulled the trigger, and they were off.

Jimmy sprinted off down the track. Looking sideways he noticed Dan, and all the other kids, were keeping up with him in a perfectly straight line. Jimmy could also see the commentators jumping up and down like demented kangaroos, with surprised looks on their faces. Jimmy's black hair was flicking up and down and his skinny legs were moving as fast as they could go, but amazingly, the other competitors were still right beside him. Jimmy crossed the finish line, but everyone in the race seemed to have finished at exactly the same time.

Everyone looked just as surprised as he did. The competitors had crossed the line at precisely the same time! He looked at Dan whose mouth looked like a goldfish's. Dan scowled at him and walked away.

Jimmy realised with disgust that EVERYONE was the winner.

How could Boris get it so wrong?!

Pandemonium broke out as everyone started to tussle for the trophy. The fire department sprayed water at the competitors, making them scatter. The principal stepped up to the podium and told them all to go home. First out of the school gates, Jimmy raced home to confront Boris.

"What did you do?" he demanded as soon as he stepped into his bedroom.

"What?" yawned Boris.

"You didn't make my wish come true!" yelled Jimmy.

"Yes I did," said Boris. "I made everyone a winner, like you said."

"No," groaned Jimmy. "I only wanted ME to be the winner."

"Oops," said Boris starting to sob. "I'm sorry. Please don't fire me into space."

"What?" asked Jimmy. "Why would I do that?"

"Because I failed you; I'm such a loser," replied Boris, wiping his eyes. "My last master said I was terrible at being a genie. To get rid of me he fired me into space, but I bounced off the International Space Station and fell back to Earth, hitting you. Truthfully I never wanted to be a genie. All I ever wanted to be was a used-car salesman, but my father wanted me to follow in his footsteps and be a genie."

Jimmy sighed. He felt sorry for Boris. He knew what it was like to be a loser. He decided for his last wish he would wish for Boris to become a used-car salesman.

Poof! In a cloud of smoke, the green mist disappeared, and suddenly Boris had legs. Boris was stunned and overjoyed.

Jimmy felt incredible too. "This is it," he said. "This is what it feels like to be a winner."

SOPHIA FOTHERINGHAM

The Chosen

I was 'Chosen'. My memory can almost grasp that night; my parent's stories gave me vision of a time when I was blind.

Golden candlelight sent the shadows retreating to the corners in fear. Strong arms cradled me, holding me tight to the two hearts that raised me. The markings I was born with, as black as the night, trailed down my face in intricate patterns. The swirls gathered at my temple and trailed off on their own pathways, down past my right eye to my chin. Hushed voices tickled my young ears when many came and watched with curious eyes as I, the first of the Chosen, slept.

I am Amber, the child born golden amongst the black night.

*

The stars looked down on the boy whom no one knew. They say he had tears of such sadness that they formed markings on his face. A shard of glass shimmered in the dim moonlight, and in the reflection he saw a young boy tracing his finger along the dark markings across his cheekbone. He too was Chosen.

He was Adam, the boy of the dark night.

I grew up alone here, an unwanted native. I stood out in the crowds. Adults frowned upon me, and children scoffed. They were uncertain of me, wary of my unusual features. I was eight when I met Adam. He was my first and only friend.

We lived in the land of Drowden. From my perch in the tree, I watched the comings and goings of the ships in the distance, bored, yet somehow intrigued. Majestic ships, made from the lands finest woods, filled the harbour, their sails fluttering like angels' wings. The gentle winds sent soft waves across the meadows around me. An inner desire rose to capture my perspective; to freeze it in time forever. A young child with rosy cheeks jogged past chuckling, mud smeared across his face, boldly insulting my markings again. A tall boy walked past him smiling, and ruffled the little boy's hair. Oh, it was Adam. Trust Adam to smile at the boy who humiliated us. Adam seemed to be constantly grinning, his face always gleaming. He was like a sun that was always glowing and never burned out, no matter what the circumstances.

Adam, was like a big brother to me. I had always wanted to capture him in time too. I could see in my mind just where the light would be, softly accentuating his bold cheekbones, where his striking markings rest, and his smile bringing joy to the entire picture. Compared to him I was dark and intimidating. I began my route down the old oak tree as I saw his amiable face come closer.

We wandered aimlessly down the cobbled street, taking it all in. We didn't know what would be thrust upon us the next day, the day of the Chosen. We were the Chosen. There were six of us, all with some form of marking. Tomorrow we would all meet for the first time.

*

My stomach was a cage filled with butterflies. Adam paced around the room with a terrifyingly straight face, making me jump with every step. We were all on edge. The four anonymous, unfamiliar faces intimidated me. The space was too large. Monumental pillars reached to the ceiling, and delicate stories of those before us twisted their way around them. There were six pillars, each with a smooth section near the bottom – a space left for our stories.

Footsteps echoed in the vast space as the author entered. "Your time has come," his gravelly voice announced. "You have twelve hours to make us like you, to show us your skills."

We stared at each other with wide eyes, each too scared to speak. Adam was the first to recover.

"May I be so bold as to ask why we have been put in this room? Why we have to make you like us, and most importantly why us?"

"You have been randomly selected by nature," the unknown man continued, "so don't begin to flatter yourselves. This room is the room in which you will spend your time. Wisely may I add. The banquet table is in the back for refreshments, and in the corner you will find all the equipment you need for skills. Remember, we will be assessing you at all times. At the end of today, the Elders and I will choose the most fitting of you to become our ruler."

Emotions charged through my body, leaving me overwhelmed by all the information. "So you mean that we are not different from anybody else, just randomly selected from normal people?" I said.

"Yes. Build a bridge and get over it, honey. It's called life," he snapped. "You may proceed." He turned sharply and walked out, leaving only the echo of his footsteps.

Adam strolled over to the corner crammed with clutter, and a luminous grin spread across his face as he picked up a massive instrument, sat down, and began to play a thrilling tune that sent shivers up my spine. The rest of us immediately felt the pressure and began to search for our skill.

A white canvas with a set of colourful paints spoke to me, and thus the day began. I isolated myself from the others, Adam's shrill melodies inspiring me from a distance. I painted all the images inside me. I painted my emotions. I painted my past, and finally I painted my future.

We had interviews and quizzes. They sent in children, the sick, and even the fighting. None of it seemed to matter. I painted so hard and with so much feeling that, when the time was up, I came out of my own little world. I felt like the chasm in which I had stored all my anger and frustration at myself – for being different – was empty. I felt new. I knew as soon as I saw Adam that he felt the same. His face was blotchy and in my head I heard the hoarse, sorrow of his story told through his cello.

*

I looked back on that time, as I painted the portrait of my joyful, humble king (also known as my best friend). I was grateful that I was Chosen. I could now express my feelings in a way special to me, and I spread that to others in our land. Growing up, children told me that I was a nobody, but through being Chosen, I've realised that it was a lie. I was just empty because I listened to what people told me. I knew that in my own way I had won, because I found myself and filled my chasm. We were no longer different, just unique; the people had grown to see past our markings, which had begun to fade.

Every now and then a child would ask why I have a birthmark on my face. I'd stop and explain.

SABINA SYSANTOS

Gold

I ran away,
from what I knew (constant, perfect, easy), in exchange for mere
chances.
I kept going no matter how many things I dropped
on the way.

I had a good thing going and still wanted more.
Running meant leaving everything behind,
But doing this for myself meant going towards a bigger prize.
There's something about a struggle
– the beauty in a tragedy.

As long as I keep running, I'll have everything I need
Because even though I've lost a lot, I still feel like I'm winning.
I'm winning because I'm on the way to where exactly
I want to be.

NADIA SNEGIREV

A Lesson for the Adults

Dear Parents and Principals
Of those kids you 'reward'
With the 'Everyone's a Winner' award.

All those expectations you conceive
On your children to do great things,
But if every parent believes
That their child is exceeding,
What does average even achieve?

Children's bags filled to the brim
With school books and stationery
And a packed lunch jammed in.
Carefully made sandwiches
Filled with standards, not cut slim,
Lies packaged in plastic wrap,
Children's future, looking grim.

The fatal blows are dealt out,
Weapon of choice – email.
Civil people shouldn't shout
Education, our warfare,
Each child, a diligent boy scout,
Every parent, a firm sergeant.
Is this what learning should be about?

So how does a school cope with this?
The Everyone's-A-Winner Award
With rainbows and stars you can't miss
Loads pre-schoolers' report envelopes,

Provides an endearing kiss
From a briefly satisfied parent,
Left for adults to reminisce.

Being the best became the norm.
It pushed kids into growing up,
Childhood became reformed.
No time to play, no time to live,
Just shoved in school uniforms
Edging towards the cliff's edge.
How could parents be so misinformed?

Can we stop this dangerous train,
Chugging along on our kids dreams?
Instead let's be humane.
Make winning on their own terms.
Only then can parents gain
The successes you would die for.
If we can all just abstain,
Everyone can be a winner
Again.

The Hunter

The moon and the stars were high, and the village slept, yet the forest was wide awake. Shadows stalked through the moonlight, and a loud snap of twigs echoed like a scream. The trees groaned as a hard gust of wind shoved against them. The forest was angry. A monster, an intruder, was entering.

He was dressed in rags. A layer of dust covered him like silk. He was thin, as thin as sticks, and had pale, sickly skin. He moved like air, soft and silent. This monster knew the forest and all its secrets. He had hunted there before. He was raised on the edge of the forest and had played there as a child.

The nightmares in the forest had haunted him for decades, the eyes in the darkness watching him every second. The forest still sent shivers of fright up his spine but he ignored them; he couldn't face those fears. He had a job. He couldn't disappoint his children by returning home empty-handed. His soul screamed to save an innocent animal's life, but saving an animal would kill his children. He couldn't run away from the darkness.

He crouched close to the earth and ignored the roar of anger from the trees above. A bead of sweat ran down his forehead. He tried desperately to quiet his breathing, but it escaped from his lungs like a rush of steam from a train. His fingers dug into the dirt and he felt small bugs slithering over his fingertips. The humid air assaulted him. His eyes darted all around, and he watched every shadow, sensing for danger and creatures. His face showed no emotion, but inside, his heart thumped like a drum. Every nerve, every hair on his body, was telling him to leave and never return. Go home, they said. Home. That was why he was here. He had to save his children: his poor, starving sons and daughters. There was no other choice.

Crunch.

The hunter's head snapped up and his gaze narrowed through the moonlight. A large, proud stag stood at the edge of a clearing, head bent, nibbling on a bit of grass. A mixture of horror and relief bubbled inside the hunter; the stag would provide dinner for a week, but would remove a life from the world forever. Slowly the hunter pulled a gun from his jacket and aimed.

Boom!

The stag reared and yelped, and the forest floor shuddered as his limp body fell.

The hunter hesitated, then began to crawl across the forest floor towards the dead stag. A tear rolled down his cheek. To the forest he was a monster, a murderer (and the hunter felt like one inside); but he was good. His love for his children out-weighed his heart and his goodness. He would do anything for his children. He was the only person in the whole world they could rely on. Without him they would have starved years ago. For them, he had to be a winner.

It only took one second for his whole world to come crashing down around him.

A cloud of smoke drifted along the forest floor, going unnoticed by the hunter. It wasn't until the smoke had seeped into his skin like claws that he caught its scent, causing a wave of pain and panic to crash through him. His screams echoed across the forest as the smoke dragged him onto his knees and completely took over his body; all he could see, taste, smell, and feel was the smoke until he was smoke himself.

Slowly, the smoke evaporated. His choked breathing was loud in his ears, his body trembling and shuddering with shock. Something was wrong. The smoke was gone; or was it? In his soul, a layer of the cloud lingered. He gasped as the smoke began to dig into his emotions, his memories, completely taking over every part of him. All his goodness, all his happiness, was gone.

But he was a hunter. He would do what hunters do: hunt.

He lifted the gun in his hands, a small, wicked smile playing on his face. He got to his feet, chuckling to himself as he swaggered out of the forest. His destination was home; the smoke inside him was telling him to remove the problems causing his poverty. His children.

He stepped out of the forest, the light of dawn catching his eyes. Rather than their normal colour of deep hazel, the light reflected a colour as red as the devil. The forest, the smoke, had turned him evil.

John

John woke up dead.

This should have been concerning to John, but as he would tell you, "It's hard to care about things when you're dead." And he had been dead for weeks.

He doesn't know how he knows this. Time is another thing that it's hard to care about while you're dead.

John lay in his bed, small piles of decaying flesh sloping off under his skin.

'I should probably start living again,' he didn't think. He didn't think about much when he was dead. He was dead.

*

John woke up alive.

This did concern him.

John woke up alive and screaming.

The scream was a booming silence. An unbearably loud non-sound that made his ears ring.

John started humming softly to quiet the silence. John didn't like silence. It reminded him of that time he died. That time was recent, but this only made the fear stronger. John seemed to care more about being dead once he was alive.

John got out of bed, brushed his perfect white teeth and cleaned his soft supple skin. He stared at the mirror until he was a different person. John still looked like John but now he was someone else. That man then went outside of the story.

Sometime later a man who wasn't John walked back into the story. He then looked at the mirror until he was John. He cried a little until he was John. John could do things the other man couldn't. The other man could do things John couldn't. They needed each other in that way. They were winners in that way; both of them, and neither. The prize was each other after all.

"A prize is just making up for the punishment," the other man would say. Over and over – a hymn for only some sins.

John brushed his perfect white teeth and cleaned his supple soft skin. And cleaned his supple soft skin. And cleaned his supple skin. And cleaned his slightly raw skin. Then he felt pain. Then he felt tears. John was crying again. John was dying again.

*

John went to sleep dead.

John woke up dead.

John didn't care about this as he was dead.

JUSTINE LIM-RANOLA

The Seas

The world teetered
on the edge of
strong-mindedness
and discrimination.

Out of balance,
cracks formed on
the planks walked
on by each nation.

Then the world fell
off the ship of
peace and into
the seas of war.

Seeking salvation,
it tried to use
violence as
a makeshift oar.

With uncertainty,
it was a fight
they felt could
never be won.

Then they stopped
and really looked.
Then realized
it could be done.

Communicating
with words instead
of firearms,
understanding began.

They swam and helped
each other until
the world ended up
washed up on the sand.

Instead of finding
peace together,
they found something
that was even greater;

The Island of
Tolerance where
the world helped
themselves become winners.

SOPHIA FOTHERINGHAM

The Once Girl

She lives in the house where ivy climbs
Where bees throb in the golden air;
They follow the dance of intricate vines
Cradling the house on the hill.

Around the house she grew up in as a girl,
The wind sent rolling waves across the meadow;
Amongst the sea of green grasses, a pearl
To her a secret that reassured.

The girl a gentle, vulnerable, creature
The mockery of children, a laughed at grotesque;
She looked ahead with the words of her teacher,
And focused on winning her game of life.

She left behind the scars of past years,
And explored the world with adult eyes;
Thin ribbons of memories that disappear,
As she buys longer, brighter, more exotic ones.

Once again here the once girl lives,
And claims the sea of meadows with her tender
hands;
To children with flowers in their braids she gives
The ribbons of the girl she once was.

She tells them as she passes on her pearls,
"Don't let the others define your ribbons;
Be what you want, because what matters girls,
Is that you win your game of life."

VICTORIA MALONEY

The Repulsive Race

They said this would be fun, that everybody's a winner.

But not me.

How can I be a winner when I am forced to run this track? Slaving away in the hot sun – for what benefit? How is it that me running the cross country will do any good? It certainly isn't for pleasure; that much I know. Why do the unathletic students have to participate? It is basically torture and is certainly a violation of human rights. But here I am, legs pumping, shorts rubbing, and fountains of sweat cascading down my body. I'm sure I look quite the sight. However, I keep on running, determined to finish this dreaded race, even though I am suffering from a severe lack of air.

I pass walkers left and right who are in an even worse state than I am. They are kids who I thought were fit, but here they are dragging themselves along the concrete in pain as they ache to cross the line and end their misery. I pity them. I am unsure that anybody would do this for fun, but in my fatigued state I am unable to come up with an accurate answer. I glance back over my shoulder at them and marvel at the long lines of stragglers in the far distance. Perhaps I'm not doing too badly then.

I grin at the thought and begin to focus on the pounding of my feet on the pavement. One, two, one, two. It's nice to focus on the calming rhythm, so that I can run at a constant speed for the rest of the race, conserving energy so that I won't burn out right at the end and let all the slow pokes get in front of me. Even if I don't want to do this race, I'm certainly not going to come last. That would be embarrassing, and my heart goes out to the poor soul who will.

Though my year doesn't seem to be an overly athletic group, they are not above making fun of the ones who come last. There will doubtless be a bit of name calling and teasing.

I am about three-quarters through the track now, and am more determined than ever to see it end. I can hear the crowds of the younger year groups cheering in the distance. All I have to do is run around this field twice, but it isn't as easy as it sounds. In fact, it's rather daunting. The field is massive and, though it is coated in a soft looking green grass, its emptiness is intimidating, as if at any moment it could swallow me whole and nobody would notice.

Swallowing my uncertainty, I start to jog around the field. My breath is becoming more unsteady. I am unsure whether it is due to the anticipation of finishing to the roar of a crowd, or because a lung is about to burst out of my body. I carry on pushing my body to its physical limits as I gallop around the paddock. One lap left to do.

A few other students have begun to run around the field. I pass them grinning, finishing my last lap. I know I only have to sprint down the road and I'll see the finish line. A surge of determination overtakes my body and I find myself exceeding what I had thought to be the limits. I fly down the footpath and soon I can see the line.

People begin to cheer and chant my name. Grinning like a Cheshire cat I cross the line. There is a teacher there waiting to take my name and record my placing. I'm not first, but I've made the top 30 at least. She congratulates me and then strolls away. Perhaps cross country isn't that bad.

People walk past and clap me on the back, congratulating me for finishing the race and getting points for my house group. Maybe, just maybe, everybody is a winner. I mean, just by passing the line I have gained points, which could help my house to win.

Admitting I was wrong, even if just to myself, is not something that comes easily. Yet today is the first day that I would actually admit to being wrong and would do so proudly, knowing that I have had a lot of fun doing something I had thought I despised.

GABRIELLA CONWAY

Moments

The Act of Equality was signed in 2505 by representatives of each nation, after more than half a century of controversy and debate. It declared that every man, woman, and child has the choice to reach their full potential, to be treated with an unbiased mind, and to establish a life that is proportional to others.

So on the night my dad died, I was given the choice to change it.

As Dad passed prematurely, given the average life span, my family was now not considered equal to others in my generation, and I had the right to change this. As Mum had already used her quota of one 'revival', it was my choice alone.

It was a split-second decision, just like when I had thrown on the brakes as Ginger – our neighbours' cat – raced across my path, resulting in me being thrown over the handlebars. It would have been life or death for that cat, and now it was my dad's.

The 'Moment' room was a wall of mirrors, but once I stood near one, it rippled and wavered like the surface of a pond. It reminded me of the teleportation system we used when travelling long distances – except instead of showing you the location of your destination, it showed your destination in time. I stepped into it. It was like walking into a pool of cool water, moving slowly as the cold seeped into your skin and goose bumps ruptured the surface.

The roar of engines snapped my eyes against the now heavy air, warm and humid in the midst of summer. The splutter of exhaust wafted in the air as slim transport machines rolled past, their weighted tyres pressing into the sunken ground. I didn't have long to wait: already my dad was nearing the track, his sweaty, straining form weaving through the wisps of haystacks.

My hands itched at my sides as the rumble of the truck neared.

The chipped teal paint was a reminder of its age and more importantly the cue I needed. The pounding in my ears increased to match my heartrate as I slipped out of the cloth suit and hid behind a nearby tree. I shivered, feeling exposed as I became visible to others. I glanced down at my watch. 3:28pm. Less than a minute to go. The timing had to be perfect, the change taking place in the minimum amount of time needed to diminish the chance of any other change occurring. The buzz against my skin alerted me to the time, and I jumped into action. Vaulting across the field I cried his name, my muscles straining with the effort.

"Dad! Dad!"

He stopped in his tracks, and I had a chance to see a flicker of bewilderment in his eyes before tyres squealed and an ear-shattering howl rang through the air. I halted in mid-stride, heart thumping in my chest.

"Stay back!" Dad cried. His eyes reflected the horror in my own.

My feet worked without my noticing, and I stumbled forward into his arms. I sobbed for my mistake and for my relief. Here was my dad, warm and safe and alive, yet a dead man lay at my feet. Another buzz near my wrist indicated I had to leave, and I pulled myself away from him. Collecting the tears from my face with my sweater I stepped back, careful not to look at his face.

"I-I should go." I tripped over my words, gulping against my sobs.

Concern was clear on his face as he watched me, touching my shoulder lightly as if to stop me from leaving.

"Will you be alright?" His eyes flickered and he looked behind me.

I nodded, shivering.

"Yeah, I just need to leave." I prayed this didn't need further explanation.

"Be careful," he said, before releasing my shoulder.

I forced myself to walk away calmly, my whole body strained. But as soon as I was out of view, I sprinted towards the clearing in the forest. The air already rippled, a sign that it was soon to close. Pain shot up my legs as they hammered against the ground; my heart was in my throat as it beat at a crescendo. I made it in the nick of time, throwing myself towards the gap with no time to prepare for the pool of coldness that ripped through my body. I was suspended, motionless, in a sea of black; all of time and all different outcomes whirled around me – everything and anything was possible in that moment.

*

I fell heavily onto a cool, steady surface. I lay, panting as waves of nausea crashed over me, my stomach heaving as it processed the change in time. I wasn't sure how long I lay there – it could have been hours or seconds – before someone pulled me off the ground and guided me to a plush couch, urging me to sip the mug of steaming liquid in front of me. I stared up at them, my vision blurred. I noticed a kind, soft face peering at me, framed by a mass of soft blonde hair. Exactly like the man I had just killed.

I collapsed against myself, wailing like a toddler. How could this be fair? Trading one life for another, surely this didn't make the world equal.

When I had no tears left to spill, a kind woman took me through to an adjoining room. In front of me was a silver box.

"You can change it, you know."

I looked up at her, my eyes wide.

"The moment you changed … that time hasn't solidified yet. That moment can still be reversed to its original state."

My heart numbed. Time could be re-written.

"But my dad will still be dead." The words felt heavy in my

mouth.

She placed a warm hand on my shoulder. "And the man that was not meant to be killed would be alive. You can save him."

My dad's life to clean the blood from my hands.

I shut my eyes. Was this the price for a world to be equal?

"How?" I asked.

I heard the click of a lock and saw the sides of the silver box fall away revealing a smooth blue button.

"One press and time will be reversed."

I released my hand from where I clutched it to my chest.

My dad lifted me up in the air.

I'm flying.

My skin bristled against the sudden cool air.

Then he was gone.

I'm falling.

My hand skimmed the surface.

Now I was a boy crying against his father's gravestone.

One movement was all it took – for time to be re-written, for the victim's life to be exchanged with my father's.

The gravestone faded and the boy's father cradled him, back from the dead.

*

So now I was fatherless and I was not equal. But the man I saved had a son and I wondered, would the boy have done the same as I? For wouldn't his life have become unbalanced too, if his father had passed?

It took my father's death for me to realise the cruel truth of my world. Even in a society that was governed equal, not everyone could be a winner.

Nothing a Little Blush Can't Fix

Daisy Ackerman sat at the living room table, wearing a garish, pearl-trimmed ball-gown and sucking her thumb. She was thinking (as most six-year-old girls do) about chocolate ice-cream with sprinkles, and her mother's approval. Daisy was not allowed chocolate ice-cream. Chocolate ice-cream made little girls fat, and fat little girls didn't win prizes.

"Listen, Daisy, you need to really – float. Watch Mommy do it. Do you see, dear? You've got to really glide across the stage." Elizabeth Ackerman had a plastic smile. It was fading fast. "Don't you see, dear? Daisy!"

Daisy did not see. Daisy was not paying attention. Unfortunately for her, Daisy had an attention span that was almost as short as her raw, stubby fingernails.

Elizabeth grabbed a hold of her daughter's shoulders, and Daisy yelped in fright.

"Must I tell you again to quit that disgusting nail biting habit of yours. It's hardly feminine. Now watch."

Daisy snatched her hands from her mouth. She widened her big brown eyes and pouted with a quivering lower lip. "But Mommy, we've been doing this for hours, and I'm hungry."

She flinched as Elizabeth gave her a hard slap across the face.

"Daisy! You know that we're on a juice cleanse; you can't eat anything for the next twelve hours or you'll bloat. Listen dear, your grandmother and your grandmother's grandmother, and even her grandmother, were all 'Little Miss Metropolis'. Every one of them!" Elizabeth leaned in close. "It's of the utmost importance you look your best tomorrow. What's the rule?"

Daisy swallowed hard. Tears dribbled down her forlorn face.

"Pretty girls are skinny girls," she whispered, and wiped her nose with her hand.

Elizabeth gave a satisfied nod. Then the smile faded from her lips. "Oh God, dear, you must stop crying. It makes your skin look simply awful, and besides you'll ruin your makeup."

Elizabeth wrenched her daughter's head up and dabbed at her blotchy face with a neatly folded tissue.

"Now stand up. Your routine is sub-par at best, and we simply can't taint the Ackerman legacy with your clumpy monstrosity of a dance." She pulled Daisy to her feet in one swift movement, and scanned her shivering body with beady eyes.

Daisy hung her head and snuffled. Goosebumps speckled her bony arms.

"You've gained weight," her mother suddenly announced with a disapproving sigh.

Daisy's snivelling became even louder.

"Oh do shut up," Elizabeth snapped. "The pageant's tomorrow morning. We can't have you looking like some over-ripe strawberry in a dress."

Daisy let out an agonised wail, her stubby fingers flew to cover her mouth, but it was too late.

Elizabeth's nostrils flared with anger. "If that's how you really felt, I wouldn't have caught you binging on that chocolate cornetto last night! That's an entire day's worth of empty calories, you stupid girl! You're an embarrassment," she spat, staring down at the shaking six-year-old.

Daisy's mascara had begun to run in mismatched rivulets down her freckled pink cheeks. "But if you never won the pageant then why do I have to?" she blurted out tearfully.

Elizabeth inhaled sharply.

Slap.

Daisy's neck jerked violently to the side, and she collapsed in a neat heap on the hardwood floor. The crying stopped.

Elizabeth cleared her throat. "Daisy?"

There was no reply.

"Come now, Daisy, you're being over-dramatic."

Daisy's long meticulously curled, bouffant hair lay limp around her flushed face. Her eyes were open. And still. The vein on Elizabeth's forehead was bulging luridly.

"You know you must get that awful blank expression off your face. It's enough of an effort to get you looking human with a little eyeshadow and lipstick, but that gaping-fish look just puts us right back where we started," Elizabeth declared with a shrill laugh.

She nudged her motionless daughter with the toe of her Louboutin.

"Honestly, Daisy. You're a girl, not a sack of flour. Act like it," she said with an edge of hysteria.

The lightbulb above them flickered faintly. Elizabeth gave Daisy a sharp kick to the ribs, and waited expectantly. There was no response. Elizabeth huffed with annoyance.

Grabbing her daughter's hand, she began to drag Daisy towards the hallway. Her head caught on a skirting board with a thump.

"Oh dear me," Elizabeth tutted, "you must be more careful."

Daisy stared back at her with sad unblinking eyes.

Her mother smiled. "I wouldn't worry, darling. It's nothing a little blush can't fix."

JOANNA LI

Paradise

cross the finish line, the ribbons flying, gold,
heavy, around your neck.

congratulate yourself.

this is my punishment.
I've made it to the promised land, belly swollen
with hate

       friends
              forgotten,
     family
             begotten,

there's no way to move
but forwards now.
keep your head high, don't look back.
there's nothing there to see.

paradise awaits,
the immortality of forever,
crystalliscd.
perfect and frozen. unchanging, unmoving,
there's nothing to fear here.

you've won.

I've made it to the promised land,
but I've made it alone.

BOBBIE RUSHTON

Dear Baby Brother

Dear Baby Brother
I never thought it could be you.
I never wanted it to be you.

Dear Baby Brother
The darkness came as fast as you got your angel wings.
My tears will never go away.
My heart feels like it's been thrown away.

Dear Baby Brother
You were my partner in crime.
Together forever.
Like lemon and lime.

Dear Baby Brother
You've always been there for me,
But now you are about to leave.
I know we fuss and fight,
But I love you with all my might.

Dear Baby Brother
I wish you were home,
It hurts me to think you're so alone.
It's not the same without you here,
Why you did what you did is still unclear.

Dear Baby Brother
I remember, together as teens
The video games you played that I thought were lame.
To fighting and arguing and all that in between,
To laughing and joking, and you thought I was being mean.

Dear Baby Brother
I remember when we were little and we played outside,
But to you that's classified.
You'd look at me with that smile
Oh, how your smile used to stretch for a mile.

Dear Baby Brother
I pray for you every night before I go to sleep,
And every time I think I hear you creep.
Sometimes it's like you're still here,
I look at the door and wait for you to appear.

Dear Baby Brother
You were a winner.
Even though you grew thinner and thinner.
You always said how "Everyone's a winner."

Dear Baby Brother
Don't leave me alone in this world.
We're related by blood.
Brother and sister.
Don't break this bond.
If only I had a magic wand,
For you to come home to your loving family.

Dear Baby Brother
You were the best.

Wired Right?

The bus was filled with the incessant chatter of fourteen teenage girls. The air was hot and stuffy, and a blast of deodorant spray from the seats in front only made things worse. Tracy and her two cronies, Fiona and Lyndsay, were giggling somewhere behind her.

Karen fished her phone out of her schoolbag. The screen read '4 missed text messages' in bold lettering, the little envelope icon bouncing up and down impatiently. All from her mum.

Her mum was a worrier, and Karen supposed that was understandable, with everything that had happened over the last few years. Two years ago, Karen had taken a sudden turn for the worse. She had stayed at the institution a lot, and just when everyone thought that she wasn't going to get better, she did. Karen had spent the last year rebuilding her life, making a few friends, getting good grades, joining the soccer team. Regular trips to a therapist helped to keep her focused. Of course, she didn't blame her mum for being concerned: sometimes Karen suspected herself of slipping, losing it. Lately, she hadn't felt quite right, but she didn't want to miss the soccer tournament, so she had dismissed it as simply being tired from training.

The bus ground to a halt beside the soccer fields. Whistles could be heard from the multiple games being played. The girls jostled their way out of the bus, giving rushed thanks to the driver. Already dressed in their red and gold stripes, they jogged towards a spot in the shade, hauling bags of soccer gear. Their first game was in half an hour, so there was no time for rest.

Karen tied her boots, and Linda, their coach, organised a warm up. The sun bathed the field in heat, lighting up the sparkles in her teammates' eyes.

With game time approaching, Linda pulled the girls into a huddle and gave her usual pep talk. "No matter the score, at the end of the day everyone's a winner if we try our best."

"Let's just hope Karen can stay on her feet this time," Tracy murmured, earning a prompt giggle from Fiona.

Karen felt heat rise to her cheeks and quickly glued her eyes to the ground.

Now in the last minute of the second half, they needed one more goal to draw. Everything came down to this. Before Karen realised what was happening, she had the ball and was sprinting, hearing cheers of encouragement on all sides. She spotted a gap, the goal was straight ahead. She took aim and shot. Or she thought she did. Fate was cold-hearted that day. The ball glanced off her boot and spun away. In disbelief, Karen skidded to a stop. The whistle blew, and the girls from the opposing team hugged and squealed. But all Karen could hear were the exasperated sighs of her teammates.

The air was thick with disappointment as they trudged back to their luggage.

"You gave it your best shot, girls," said Linda. She gave Karen's back a pat. Karen just wanted to go home; this game had meant the world to her team. She could sense eyes drilling holes in her back, and risked a look behind her to see Tracy's group, heads together, muttering.

The girls went to watch a game, but Karen didn't feel like being around the others. She saw that Tracy was still packing up. Taking a deep breath, Karen crossed over to her.

"Hey Tracy, sorry about that," she started cautiously.

"Oh, it's fine. Next time, right?" said Tracy as she walked away. An innocent enough response, but the icy undertone betrayed her true feelings.

"Yeah, I guess," Karen mumbled.

The girls returned for lunch. Megan was complaining of a sprained ankle, meaning she was off for the remaining games.

"Maybe when you're better, you could go on for Karen. She couldn't even kick the ball, poor thing," said Tracy, her voice laced with false kindness.

"Yes, she's not functioning at full capacity, is she?" said Fiona.

"She probably needs new batteries," Lyndsay giggled.

"Waste of perfectly good batteries," said Tracy, "especially for something that's not wired right."

The group erupted into laughter.

Something stirred deep inside Karen, something that wanted to break to the surface. Karen got up and ran, their cruel sniggers echoing in her ears long after she left.

She wiped the tears from her face, and rested her thumping forehead against the cool wall of the cubicle. Eyes closed tightly, she tried the breathing patterns her therapist had taught her, but it wasn't working. Her breath came in ragged, angry gasps that seemed to tear at her lungs and throat.

Karen felt something snap in her mind. Something changed, in the way that everything went hot, in the way that her muscles tightened, in the way that her fists clenched, turning her knuckles white. She shot to her feet with a sudden, irrepressible need to move, to act upon this new feeling. Except it wasn't new. It had just been lying dormant, like a silent, dangerous animal, poised to strike.

She paced inside the cubicle, hot tears streaking down her cheeks. Rage built and built: it felt like her chest was going to explode. She swung her fist into the wall, hearing but not feeling the crunch of the impact. Split knuckles cried with Karen, red tears that wound their way around her fingers and dripped onto the floor.

With a contrasting calmness, she exited the cubicle and let cold water from the sink soothe her injured hand. She paused as someone entered the bathroom.

"Well, this really is pathetic. Hiding in the bathroom, Karen. Seriously, are you five?" Tracy strutted to the mirror to fix her ponytail.

Karen's hands trembled, eager, at her sides.

Tracy examined Karen's face. "Oh my God, you've been crying!" She laughed. "You should go back to primary school; maybe you'd fit in there." Tracy adjusted her uniform. "Oh who am I kidding? You wouldn't fit in anywhe –"

Karen grabbed the girl's ponytail, and with one swift movement, smashed Tracy's head into the corner of the sink. Tracy collapsed, holding her broken, bleeding nose.

"What are you doing, you freak!" Tracy screamed, but Karen couldn't hold back her anger anymore. It felt too good to release the pressure that had piled up in her head. Tracy's look of fury morphed into one of terror. Suddenly Karen was surrounded by jeering, faceless figures. Words of ridicule swirled in her mind.

"Noooooooooooooo!" Karen covered her ears, but the laughter echoed around her skull. She realised she had to silence it herself. Her hands, slick with warm blood, snaked around Tracy's neck.

It could have been minutes, or hours, but she didn't loosen her hold until the sound of laughter seeped away into the corners of her mind. Her breathing heavy, Karen pushed herself off Tracy's motionless body. Her vision blurred as she climbed to her feet.

*

She heard someone enter the bathroom.

"Well, this really is pathetic. Hiding in the bathroom, Karen. Seriously, are you five?" Tracy strutted to the mirror to fix her ponytail.

Karen's hands trembled, eager, at her sides.

Up for Auction

Samuel Poole was gliding through the countryside in his 1964 Ford Falcon, gazing straight ahead in an obnoxiously lazy fashion. One hand gripped the steering wheel, his other rested possessively on the black briefcase in the passenger seat. He passed a sign on his right that read. 'Welcome to Jackson, Mississippi: City with Soul!'

Samuel was travelling around the country, visiting Evangelical Protestant Churches in the southern Bible Belt. Right now, he was heading to Jackson for an audience with Reverend James of the Jackson City Baptist Church, where he would be conducting an auction – of sorts. He was asking churches to place bets on the contents of his briefcase: his soul.

The case actually held a contract formulated by Samuel and his lawyer, that handed over Samuel Poole's soul to whoever signed it. Before this, Samuel had been dead broke. In debt actually. After his mother died, he had escaped his highly religious home town in the south and had moved out to Vegas. He had made a living in not-so-honest ways that had him in over his head and scrambling for a way out, before he got into a great deal of trouble with the law.

He had been watching a documentary on T.V. one night about Codex Gigas, the devil's bible. The legend tells the tale of a monk who sold his soul to the devil in order to write it. That got Samuel thinking. Could he sell his soul? He had talked to a lawyer and as it turned out, he could.

He parked in the church's car-park and headed to the main building. The air carried to him the delicate notes of a hymn being played. He caught notes of singing, passionate yet soft; it was an almost haunting reminder of his childhood.

*

He had attended a church much like this one: all fancy spires and pillars adorned with crosses. A good boy, he went every week without fail. He said his prayers and believed in God with all his heart. He had believed that he could feel God looking down at him, watching over him. He felt all his sweet little prayers being answered. But Samuel could also remember the exact moment when he first felt that God had turned his back on him.

His mother was lying in a hospital bed, her frail body swathed in white sheets. Tiny tubes grew from her hands and snaked up to where they connected to clear bags of fluid hanging from metal poles. Eighteen-year-old Samuel and his father sat by her side in silence, praying. Suddenly they heard her feeble voice whispering to them.

"Samuel ..."

Samuel rushed to his mother's side and grasped her hand. She raised it to her lips and kissed it gently.

"Mother!"

"Samuel, I love you. I love you so much."

The nurses left Samuel and his father alone in the cold hospital room for a while.

He knelt by his mother's limp body and wept. His father sat on his chair, hunched over with his head in his hands. Samuel couldn't tell if he was praying or crying.

Samuel begged God to give him his mother back. He had had no idea how he could live without her. But God didn't reply.

That made Samuel wonder how someone, who was supposed to be so good, let such terrible things happen to people who didn't deserve them.

*

A receptionist wearing a hostile expression sat at a cramped desk in the foyer. Samuel walked up to her and told her that he had a four o'clock appointment with Reverend James. She told him coldly to follow her. They walked down a hallway until they reached a door labelled, 'Reverend James – Senior Pastor, Head of Finances, and T.V Personality.' The receptionist knocked before turning on her heels and walking back the way they had come.

A rich, booming voice bade him enter. At a large wooden desk sat a stern looking man, clothed in black and wearing an unreadable expression.

Samuel shook hands and introduced himself, before sitting down opposite the Reverend. He coughed and adjusted his tie, feeling beads of sweat growing at his temples. He dug his nails into his palms and began.

"Reverend James, you know why I am here. You believe that men have no right over their souls: that they belong entirely to God. Perhaps you believe that a man should have no control over his soul. You feel it is your duty to save a soul if the opportunity is presented to you. So I offer you this: my soul, in its entirety, with full and limitless control over it, to turn it over to God, as is your duty. I am a sinner, but my soul can be saved."

As Samuel said this, the Reverend's eyes flashed with things that Samuel recognised: curiosity, desire, fear. Fear was a toy that Samuel could play with.

"Of course, you may wonder what will happen if you turn down my offer. Someone else shall come into possession of my soul. Who knows what they would do with it? What would God think of that, of you casting aside an opportunity? I highly doubt that he would be pleased."

The Reverend spoke hurriedly, his eyes gleaming in terror. "How do I know that your offer is genuine?"

"In my briefcase," – Samuel gestured to the black attaché case to his right – "are all of the legal documents concerning this. If you do place the highest bid, our lawyers may meet to discuss the authenticity of them."

"Bid?"

"Oh, yes. You see, I am running an auction. Various people from all over the country have placed bids on my soul. Whoever places the highest shall be able to sign my contract and be in full legal possession of my soul. The current highest is 1.5 million U.S. dollars, placed by a church in Texas."

"Well, I shall bid two million!"

"Two million. Will the members of the church agree with this spending of their money?" Samuel was sceptical that a church could make that much money, even one of this size.

"They will agree that it is the Lord's command, and that we should therefore put it first."

"Perfect! You will just have to sign a document saying that you placed the bid."

"Yes, yes. Anything."

*

Samuel was lounging in the sun, listening to the water slosh against the sides of his pool. It had been two months since he had bought this mansion in California. He spent most days trying not to remember the auction, or anything before it. But the hollow feeling in his chest wouldn't let him forget that he had cheated people out of their money. He liked to tell himself that the deal had been good for them, that they had saved his soul and were going straight to Heaven.

Samuel still believed in Heaven. He liked to think that his mother was watching him from up there. He knew she wouldn't approve of him selling his soul, but he fancied that maybe this way it was up there with her.

JACOB JONES

Two, Eight, Thirteen, Twenty-four, Thirty-four, Forty

Two, eight, thirteen, twenty-four, thirty-four, forty.

This random string of numbers will mean nothing to most people, but it meant a hell of a lot to the people of Harrow Lake. My home town of less than a thousand people didn't have a lot to be happy about. The closing of our only mill meant a lot of poor people struggling to make ends meet. But it was ok for some like the Mills family, who owned that big house across the lake from us.

Inequality was a key problem in our town. The council kept promising they would try to fix it, but they never did. My family was not poor, but we certainly weren't the Mills family. People like the Mills family didn't hang out with my lot. My dad and his mates were getting pissed up at Cheeky's Bar, while the rich people got pissed up at the Harrow Lake Country Club. My brother and I didn't have a membership, but we would sometimes break the segregation briefly.

For all their riches, the Harrow Lake upper class did not have a major focus on security. So when me and my big brother opened a fence here and there, we didn't get anything for it. We didn't steal anything – nothing like that. But we looked at our betters and I could tell my brother was seething with jealousy. I have to admit now that I was jealous too.

The food they had put on at the country club looked like something off TV. The only time I had seen people dressed as well, was when I went to my nan's funeral. Men and women laughed and talked with each other loudly; children sat at tables, being civilised. It occurred to me while we were watching that you could see almost the same thing down at Cheeky's. The only difference between the two was what they were wearing. They were both loud, and maybe at Cheeky's the kids would be running around rather than eating at a table like grown-ups. Maybe it's the place that makes the person, not the other way round.

As we were walking home, chewing identical sticks of purple gum, my brother and I talked about the club and how it wasn't as good as Cheeky's. We were lying to each other though, and we both knew it. Cheeky's was an old bomber, compared to the sports car that was the country club. When my brother and I got home we went straight to bed, thinking about that club and what it would be like to get in.

The Crazy Lottery Draw was new to the country and had only been going for a month. It was sponsored by some old American guy who had decided his money would be best used in a lottery. He didn't mention that he would be making most of the profit from the tickets, but his prize was the biggest you could get, so no one was complaining.

The draw was set at 500 million the day my mum bought her first ticket. She had always said the lottery was a scam, but apparently, if the scam was good enough, anyone would try for it. My dad had also secretly got a ticket, and I guess pretty much everyone in town had bought one. My parents got home around the same time and showed each other their tickets. They both laughed their heads off when they saw it.

That night we sat down as a family to watch the usual sitcoms. One of my favourite shows was interrupted by Dad changing the channel. A man with a fake smile plastered all over his face was talking about the lottery; he motioned to a pretty girl to pull the numbers out.

The first number out was a 2; my parents both giggled nervously. The second number that came rocketing out the machine was an 8, and my parents laughed again as if we were watching a comedy. They stopped laughing when the next two numbers that came out matched their tickets. When 34 came out of the machine, my parents fell into a scary sort of silence. The last number seemed to roll out of the machine in slow motion. The pretty girl picked it up and showed it to the camera. A big 40, proud and bold, stood out across our TV screen.

There was a moment of complete and utter silence before my dad said a word he had never used in front of us. My mum jumped off the couch and started having some sort of happy spasm. I thought she was in trouble for a second, then she hugged my dad and I knew something else was going on.

"We won!" she screamed, as I jumped up too. My brother and I were giving off big high fives and hugging each other.

When we stopped to have a breather, we heard next door going nuts. The neighbour came running over to Dad and informed him that he was a bloody millionaire. My dad was confused, but then realised that the neighbour must have won too. Over the next few hours we got calls from all over town. We were winners too, they would all say.

By the next morning, it was a strange time; everyone was crazy with joy. The news reported that every resident in Harrow Lake had picked the winning numbers. A statistician was on the news having a heart attack, saying that it should have been impossible.

Everyone won something. That meant my family didn't get the full prize – no one did. The prize was split evenly between all the winners. Which meant that while everyone won, they didn't get a huge prize. Five hundred thousand is a lot of money, but it's not enough to quit your job. My parents weren't complaining. My dad bought a Holden and he suped it up.

We pulled into the country club, pulling burnouts in the car, smoke rising from the concrete.

An old man wearing a black suit frowned as we pulled up. "They can't be here. They're … they're losers," he stuttered.

My dad walked up to him. "No, mate, no losers here. I don't know if you've heard, but everyone's a winner."

We all laughed at that. It was true: the rich folks, the poor folks, the old, the young, black and white – everyone was a winner.

White

The soles of my boots never leave this trench. This little crevice in the earth has become my whole world. I ache to stand up and stretch, to exercise my vocal cords, or to feast, but some primitive part of me holds me back. It becomes harder and harder each day to see why survival is important. I check my measly arsenal of weapons again, and glance at my more impressive array of cuts and bruises.

I risk exposing my eyes and forehead to gunfire to study the enemy. I note with surprise that no new fortifications have been constructed under the cloak of darkness the previous night.

Defences are constantly being constructed, both against the enemy and in our hearts, hardening us against the horrors of war.

My commander claims, 'Every inch of land gained is worth every drop of blood spilt.'

I'm not sure whether that remark referred to the enemy's blood or ours, but if either of those interpretations were true, then this bloody war would have been over many months ago.

The enemy is probably planning an attack. I think I can already smell the blood, and I swear I can hear the wails of despair from 'home' – not as far away from the battlefield as we thought. A surge of adrenaline should course through my veins at this realisation, but death has incorporated itself quite nicely into my daily routine. I think of warning my commander, but I know that a sentry will have already informed him, and that he will most likely come to the same conclusion himself. Besides, he would have me flogged if I attempted to give him advice. An assault on his superiority, he would say.

Such pride is what prolongs this dreadful war. Both sides have negotiated what I believe to be fair and acceptable cease-fire conditions, but it is the pride of our nation, and the pride of each individual who belongs to that nation, that refuses to let us bow down, even for the greater good. To me, it does not matter whether we can keep this flag, or the song of our nation, if in return the lives of a few men who were ripped apart from their families could be restored. What is a piece of music that has not been sung with heart for months in comparison to the mutilated corpses that lie decaying not so far away from me? Would we rather keep a scrap of dyed cloth that flies tattered on a pole and sacrifice hundreds of lives?

The answer to that question is 'Yes'.

This is the final stand. Here, the remains of both forces clash, and behind us lie our families. Families that find anxiety shooting at them day and night. Some bedroom doors that will never be opened again. Many rectangles that shall be dug into the ground.

The country that lies behind me is no better place than on the battlefield right now. They cut the mouldy crusts off their bread, and delight in scavenging some rotten vegetables. Not a morsel of meat can be found, not even for the rich and noble. Dairy is a hard-won delicacy.

At least here at the front we have a reasonable amount of canned food, and with every day that passes there are fewer mouths to feed. I wager that we'll die before our food stores run out.

My weary eyes can barely see properly, and my brain is muddled. So when I see it, I most certainly do not believe it. I do not trust my eyes, nor my mind. What a life.

A flash of pure, untainted white pierces the reds, browns, and artificial greens that cloud the distant horizon. My throat makes an odd semi-shriek as my mind finally registers and recognises the implications that the flag brings. Now, the adrenaline starts surging through my veins, something that hasn't happened in a while.

The man who leads the procession catches my eye. He marches proudly, and behind him flow the meagre remains of his force. He does not falter. He does not cry. He does not wallow in the depths of despair. The others show no such valour. Their shoulders are hunched, defeat etched into the creases in their once hopeful faces. It seems they have forgotten the sky exists; their gazes are permanently cast downwards.

I do not blame them. They march towards an uncertain future, one where they may die before the sun does tonight. They march towards a life where they may have little hope, their only solace a few scribbled words on a scrap of paper. Not only do they hand themselves over on a platter: the fate of the ones they love garnish the plate with fancy herbs and sauces.

Is courage what it takes to charge the enemy with a gun, and to fire at young and untrained soldiers as you bellow war cries? To kill the scared and sleepy requires only a callous heart. To march towards defeat with your head held defiantly high and your trembling hands giving you away – that is the epitome of heroism. To fly that flag is to float your fate upon the breeze, and hope to visit all the places you need to before the wind dies down. One does not hand over one's life to the whims of nature, much less to the whims of men.

The men that gaze at us with misty eyes and quivering knees have done what we could not. They have saved hundreds of lives. I do not think the magnitude of this hits them.

Our men laugh rowdily and drop their weapons in celebration as the solemn procession ambles ever closer. In their state of euphoria, they forget the horrors that they have committed, the lives they have stolen, the pain they have wrought. They are filed away into the archives of memory. But some of our wiser men continue to man their cannons. I tighten my finger around the trigger where the paint has been worn away to reveal the glinting steel underneath.

He does not falter in his path, and therefore nor do those who follow him. He gives the flag a gentle wave, and then allows it to fight its own battle against the breeze. The white flag becomes more visible on the distant horizon, and with it the first few rays of the sun's radiance pierce through the oppressive clouds.

The cheering in our trench becomes deafening. We have won the war.

But they have won something much, much more.

Judging Comments

Junior Poetry: *Emma Shi*

First Place: Dancing in the Dusk Sunlight by *Melissa Blackett*

Melissa Blackett sets up a beautiful landscape straight from the beginning, and this is what drew me into her poem 'Dancing in the Dusk Sunlight'. The simply stated description of houses, that 'light up one by one', smoothly sets up the transition from day to night. The array of senses — from sound to sight to smell — creates the single image of a blissful dancer, an image that stuck in my head even after I finished the poem. I felt that the end lost a little of this momentum that the beginning had, but overall, it was a poem full of lovely imagery.

Second Place: I Am Not by *Neesha Dixon*

'I am not' by Neesha Dixon was a strong poem with a captivating message of self-confidence. I loved the little specks of imagery throughout; these delicate moments were a nice contrast against the narrator's sturdy statements. I especially enjoyed the description of thoughts that 'flutter in my head like galaxies swirling around the universe'. However, I found that the last stanza was lacking this kind of description and I would have loved to see more. Still, an enjoyable piece.

Third Place: The Once Girl by *Sophia Fotheringham*

Sophia Fotheringham begins crafting the environment around her main character in 'The Once Girl'. This approach made the poem easy to follow once she moved to the description of the girl herself. As well as this, she transitioned from describing the girl's external traits to the internal. I enjoyed the steady rhythm of the piece but felt that the lovely rolling descriptions petered out towards the end. Nevertheless, I found it to be a lovely poem.

Highly Commended: I Am Pluto by *Victoria Sun*

'I am Pluto' is an imaginative piece by Victoria Sun that zooms outwards from the sun, listing the planets as they go by. Writing in the perspective of the planet Pluto itself was a nice touch, and effectively conveyed the loneliness of the little planet. Sometimes, however, I felt like words were slotted in just for the purpose of rhyme, compromising the description a little. Overall, a nice poem that presents the solar system as a wide survey of planets.

Senior Poetry: *Emma Shi*

First Place: I am Waiting for You by *Stella Jean Stevens*

'I am Waiting for You' is both the title and first line in Stella Jean Stevens' poem and it is a sharp beginning that defines the rest of the piece. The first stanza is crafted with a series of clear images, forming pictures of who or what this narrator could be: a quick creature moving through the forest undergrowth. However, near the end, the pace of the poem seemed to slow down, just as the action really began with the appearance of lights and the sound of a gun. Still, a vivid piece with a strong focus and vision in mind.

Second Place: Paradise by *Joanna Li*

Joanna Li's 'Paradise' is, at first, light and effervescent like its title, with a description of 'ribbons, flying, gold, heavy around your neck'. What makes her poem interesting is how she proves that there is no such thing as a perfect paradise; there are elements of the bittersweet too. However, the switch from first person to second person was a little confusing. So sectioning out these two different perspectives, such as placing one section in italics, could help. Overall, it was an atmospherically cohesive poem that I really enjoyed.

Third Place: Gold by *Sabina Sysantos*

'Gold' by Sabina Sysantos describes the sensation of running in the hope of something better. I enjoyed the small insert in brackets — '(constant, perfect, easy)' — which conveyed the rush of the narrator's thoughts in a way that was simple and effective. I would have loved more of these small descriptions throughout the poem, since they added touches of detail to the piece. It was definitely a nice take on the theme.

Highly Commended: Madness by *Sophie Sun*

I loved how 'Madness' by Sophie Sun was set out as a prose poem rather than the classic structure of verse. Using age as markers of time was a nice way of bringing the reader along from one development to the other. This way of covering a large breadth of time meant that the reader didn't get lost among the jumps in age. Although some phrases felt clichéd, it was still a sweet little piece on the concept of winning in relation to love.

Junior Prose: *Jan Goldie*

First Place: White by *Victoria Sun*

Victoria takes us on an intense and sobering journey into the realities of war, from the point of view of a soldier on the front line. Visceral imagery and excellent attention to detail encapsulates the futility and horror of what has obviously been a drawn out and exhausting conflict. I particularly liked the line, 'A surge of adrenaline should course through my veins at this realization, but death has incorporated itself quite nicely into my daily routine.' With expertly written phrases like this, we are transported into a world where hope is almost lost. However, the writer structures her short fiction perfectly, leading the reader to a point of despair before handing over what is ultimately a very satisfactory ending for the story and for peace as a whole. Congratulations, Victoria. This is beautifully written and imagined. I look forward to reading more from you in the future.

Second Place: Cloud Your Integrity by *Audrey Vitero*

Audrey's story reads like a fable and the language she chooses supports this choice. The piece has a pleasing sense of rhythm and is structured in a traditional manner. Perhaps in some pieces of writing, this would be seen as predictable. However, Audrey's fine understanding of her main character, a talent for creating his unique voice and efficient use of dialogue, transforms her tale by making us care about Emil's choices. The moral of the story is subtly and brilliantly brought to life as the hero holds true and the reader gets the satisfying ending we hoped for. A well-written piece with strong themes and solid characterization. Well done, Audrey.

Third Place: The Disastrous Combination of my Nan and the Mall
by *Gianna Lill*

What a great opening sentence! Gianna's concise style of writing and expert use of dialogue is the perfect platform for what is a truly humorous story. Writing in the first person gives this pacey piece a sense of immediacy, as the reader is taken on a ride full of surprises. Short, punchy sentences give momentum to the action, and there is a definite sense of place. We know exactly what country we're in from relevant use of slang and local references. Gianna leaves us hanging at the end with what is a lovely, staccato use of language that echoes the action. Great rhythm and timing, Gianna, and a well written, funny piece overall. Well done!

Highly Commended: The Winning Wish by *Caelen Kinley*

An interesting take on the theme and a humorous way to deal with what is a traditional tale – the genie and the three wishes. What starts out in the conventional way, moves through a series of twists and unexpected turns that asks the reader to question what they would do in the main character's shoes. Some snappy dialogue, funny lines, and a satisfying ending makes this a very enjoyable story. Good job, Caelen!

Senior Prose: *Jan Goldie*

First Place: Nothing a Little Blush Can't Fix by *Helena Andrews*

From the very first sentence, Helena skilfully crafts what is a subtle horror story of stolen youth. Strong, harrowing images that offer a truly awful reality for a six-year-old are made even more poignant by the writer's attention to detail. A favourite line is 'Unfortunately for her, Daisy had an attention span that was almost as short as her raw, stubby fingernails.' Efficient dialogue captures Daisy's mother's diva complex perfectly and exposes her for the monster she is. Carefully chosen adjectives, neatly lined up in short, snappy sentences, drive the action forward at a good pace, keeping us engaged and cringing at every turn. A wonderful a piece of writing that fascinates and terrifies simultaneously. Congratulations, Helena. This is a well-deserved win!

Second Place: Learning to Win by *Emma Uren*

Well-defined characters and wonderful world building make Emma's story a strong entry. In a futuristic version of our world, the tale begins by introducing some fun technology when our main characters are running late on a normal school day. However, tension builds and the sense of threat is keenly felt as the writer introduces us to the 'burgs'. There is something extremely creepy about the 'burgs' – an alien or robotic race that have taken over presumably more than just the education system – and Emma's clever weaving of back story using a retro reference to Daleks from *Dr Who*, sums it up nicely. The reader is drawn into this unique and detailed world. An engaging, interesting story that could be further developed into a longer work. Well done.

Third Place: Two, Eight, Thirteen, Twenty-Four, Thirty-Four, Forty by *Jacob Jones*

A likeable, first person narrator gives this piece it's quirky personality and unique voice. We see the small town of Harrow Lake through the keen observations of our unnamed main character. The writer has a strong sense of place and introduces the setting in a way that draws the reader in, transporting us to this isolated township and making us care about the folk who live there. Natural, colloquial dialogue, skilful use of short, punchy sentences to build tension around the lottery announcement and ultimately a very satisfying ending makes this a great story. Good job, Jacob!

Highly Commended: Lady Liberties in a Line by *Jordan Holmes*

Jordan's story stands out for many reasons, but I was most impressed by the beautiful use of descriptive language to set the scene. Just a few of my favourite phrases: the 'matronly croon of our local choir' and '… released the enticing smell of sugar which unfurled, in tendrils, across the neighbouring storefronts and distilled through the fairground.' The reader is thrown into an intriguing world of fairground mystery and false hope. We're at one with the narrator as he delights in his small rebellion against disapproving grownups and although the villain is eventually dethroned, it's almost as if the victory is bitter sweet. A fascinating piece of writing. Well done, Jordan. Keep writing.

Judging Panel:

Emma Shi

Emma Shi was the winner of Senior Poetry for *Write Off Line 2013*. She was also the winner of the National Schools Poetry Award 2013 and her work has been published in literary journals such as *Landfall*, *Poetry NZ*, and *Starling*. She is currently studying Classics and English at Victoria University of Wellington.

Jan Goldie

Bay of Plenty based author Jan Goldie's latest creation, *Brave's Journey*, has just been published by IFWG Publishing Australia. It is a fantasy adventure about a boy called Brave and a girl named True, who travel through a magical world of forests, deserts, strange creatures and ruthless soldiers, going months without a bath as they battle to save their land from the evil ruler, Mallevia. Jan loves coffee, raspberries and champagne, so she wouldn't last long on that journey. Find out more at **www.jangoldie.com**.

Editors:

Jean Gilbert

Award winning speculative writer Jean Gilbert moved from Virginia, U.S. to New Zealand in 2005, and has since called the Waikato Valley (the Shire) her home. Jean's latest work, co-authored with William Dresden, is a modern young adult fantasy called *Light In My Dark*, a tale of love, betrayal, and self-discovery. Jean's science fiction novels, *Shifters*, *Ardus*, and *The Vault* from *The Vault Agency Series*, are published by Rogue House Publishing. You can find her short story *Blonde Obsession* in *Baby Teeth: Bite Size Tales of Terror* published by Paper Road Press, and *Pride* in *Contact Light Anthology*. (**www.jeangilbert.com**)

Jean works in close association with Alessi Films, writing screenplays for promotional advertising and television.

Jean is a Core member of Speculative Writers of New Zealand (**www.specfic.nz**), and the coordinator for SpecFicNZ Central.

Chad Dick

Chad Dick, a professional editor and proofreader, lives in Katikati in the Bay of Plenty and works for 100% Proof Ltd (**www.100percentproof.co.nz**). He enjoys assisting others with their writing projects, and loves the positive interactions with authors and writers. In his spare time, he is also a writer of both fiction and non-fiction, and is currently working on a book about global environmental problems.

Cover Art:

Kodi Murray

Kodi Murray is a freelance designer/illustrator currently studying for a Bachelor of Media Arts at Wintec. Kodi is just branching into the commercial field where his talents and passions lie. Building his artistic portfolio, Kodi's work has ranged from commissions for friends, to a commission for a local celebrity, to featuring in the 2015 documentary *Reelside* for The Movie Network (Canada).

These and all of Kodi's personal works are viewable online at **www.behance.net/KodiMurrayNZ**.

Project Manager:

Piper Mejia

Piper Mejia, an advocate for New Zealand writers and literature, was the co-editor of *Write Off Line 2012* and *2013*, and *Beyond ... 2012* and *2013*; collections of writing by New Zealand intermediate and secondary students, and continues to manage both national writing competitions. In 2014 her short story *Lockdown* (included in the horror flash fiction collection *Baby Teeth: Bite-Sized Tales of Terror*) was shortlisted for the Sir Julius Vogel Award for science fiction and fantasy writing, and her young adult novella, *The Fence*, appeared in *Conclave: A Collection of Science Fiction and Fantasy*. The same year, she won a national poetry competition for her poem *Sounds of Evolution*. In 2015, her novella *Mika* (co-written with Lee Murray) won the Paper Road Press Shortcuts competition published in the inaugural Shortcuts series in 2015. In her spare time, she is a high school English teacher.